I'LL BE ALONE FOR CHRISTMAS

KRISTIN MULLIGAN

To anyone who has a wild—if not slightly
paranoid—imagination, too.

I'LL BE ALONE FOR CHRISTMAS

TABLE OF CONTENTS & PLAYLIST

I'LL BE ALONE FOR CHRISTMAS

TABLE OF CONTENTS & PLAYLIST

AUTHOR'S
NOTE

D ear Readers,
        Confused about this new-ish book? Let me
explain.

I originally released this last year under the pen name
Meyer Matthews. At that time, I was apprehensive about
publishing under my real name and wanted the creative
freedom to write an old-school slasher novella without
worrying about what readers would think of my imperfect
main character. I also tend to jump between genres, which
can be challenging for authors whose audiences prefer a
single genre.

This isn't your typical thriller novella that wraps up
nicely in a perfect red bow—pun intended. I aimed to craft
something thrilling and a bit scary—ideal for an evening

1

read by the fire with a cup of hot cocoa while wrapped in a cozy blanket.

Now, almost a year later, I feel it's time to republish this story under my real name—a story I'm proud of and had so much fun writing. *I'll Be Alone For Christmas* is a suspenseful thriller filled with disturbing scenes and a touch of gore, so proceed with caution!

Also, while Frosthaven Falls may seem picturesque and perfect for a snowy vacation, it's a fictional town you won't find on any map.

Happy reading and happy holidays!

Love,

Kristin Mulligan

CHAPTER 1

IT'S THE MOST WONDERFUL TIME OF THE YEAR

I didn't plan on being alone on Christmas. It just kind of happened.

And by happened, I mean my long-term boyfriend of two years decided he wanted to ring in 2025 as a single man instead of *ringing me in* as his fiancée.

He sat me down the week before we were supposed to leave for our anniversary getaway—the one where I thought he'd surprise me with a two-carat diamond from his back pocket on Christmas Eve and declare, "Romee, you're the best thing that ever happened to me. Will you make me the happiest man in the world and marry me?"

He'd pop some expensive champagne, and we'd make love every day until we were forced to check out of the quaint, remote cabin I'd rented.

Instead, that talk went something like this: "Romee, I'm not in love with you anymore. I don't think we were meant to be together."

I was terror-stricken, frozen, and unable to defend our dying relationship that was supposed to be my forever.

It took a whole day for me to reach out and finally say what needed to be said.

"You're making a huge mistake. We're soulmates, meant for each other!"

His mind was made up.

I think the blindsided feeling was what hurt the most; that we were on two different pages. Hell, we were in two different books. To not sense a breakup coming, to not feel the tension and discontent, to not suspect infidelity or something amiss, and then one day the person you love is just…gone? Not only is it heartbreaking—it's humiliating.

And because of this last-minute relationship tragedy, the trip I was so excited to go on, the one where we'd wake up in each other's arms for those six blissful days, was still happening with or without him by my side.

I had immediately emailed the owner of the rental and begged for a refund.

"I don't think we're able to make it. Is there a chance someone else could take my dates and I could get the deposit back?"

Linda, the owner, was kind and understanding, but rules were rules. There's a special cancellation policy around holidays, and I was well past the deadline. I'd be losing out on nearly a thousand dollars.

Then came the frantic, if not guilt-ridden, texts to my friends.

"Want to come with me? You don't even have to pay. I'll provide everything. Just come along for the views and company. I'm single! Don't make me go alone."

All my teacher friends had their winter breaks planned out well before the school year even began. We relish those two weeks of solitude away from our classroom, so it made sense no one was able to go on a last-minute whim. They had trips of their own to take, happy memories to be made.

The rest of my friends had kids and spouses of their own, and my mom was too far away and "too old" to make it in time for my wintery excursion.

The first day of my winter break was spent trying to figure out where everything had gone wrong, then deciding if I really wanted to go on this trip by myself.

I could either sit at home and cry about the future that had slipped through my fingers, while paying for the cabin, or I could sit at the cabin and mourn the relationship I thought I'd had but clearly didn't.

My friends were sympathetic and supportive.

"Don't let him ruin your life and *your Christmas!"* was the go-to phrase repeated over and over until it was stuck in my brain.

I had to get out of my apartment. I could not be more grateful that we never moved in together. I couldn't imagine packing up my things while "It's The Most Wonderful Time Of The Year" played on the radio.

The solitude was just what I needed.

Time to clear my head, figure out how I'd move on from this disaster, and get through a very blue Christmas.

B efore I booked this trip, I scoured vacation websites, looking for the perfect place to spend the holiday. Did I want something tropical? Remote? In a big city?

No, I wanted something off the grid with a peaceful, snowy ambiance. A place where no one existed but me and Landon. The cabin I settled on was a two-story home in dire need of some upgrades, but it had the three things I was looking for: a fireplace, huge bathtub, and an amazing view.

It was also within my budget and one of the few left that had the specific dates I was looking at. Did we—excuse me—*I* need the three bedrooms? No. Did I mind there was low cell service and the interior was outdated? Eh. Was it a big deal that it wasn't exactly close to civilization? At the time, no. Now, it mattered more, but it was too late.

I was going alone. So what?

I could catch up on all the television shows I never finished, maybe read a few books by the fire, do yoga on the wraparound porch if it wasn't below freezing, or take a hot bath and truly learn what it meant to disconnect–because while there was a Wi-Fi router, cell service was spotty, so the reviewers said. And there weren't many reviews at all.

I could also live my teenage years over again: stay up all night and sleep all day. Or day drink. I was away from my students, with no responsibilities, and no one to tell me how I could spend my precious time.

When the owner sent me the confirmation email the night prior to leaving, she also left the unique code to open the front door. The cleaning company would be there in the morning to ensure it was ready for new guests, and the code would only work after three p.m.

Linda was apologetic in her emails about the cancellation policy, but she promised the week would be perfect. I didn't mention I was going alone, because despite the town being charming and quaint, she didn't need to know the party of two was now a single, lonely old maid.

I decided to keep up the illusion I was a thirty-two-year-old woman going to a remote cabin in an unfamiliar town...with her boyfriend.

CHAPTER 2

I'M DREAMING OF A WHITE, RED, & ROSÉ CHRISTMAS

F rosthaven Falls lies at the top of a mountain, eight thousand feet above a bustling city. While it has a gas station, a stop-and-grab shop, and some mom-and-pop restaurants, it's a population of two thousand. Not a ton of people, if you don't count the travelers coming to ski and snowboard their impressive slopes.

There's no Starbucks, Target, or grocery store chain up there. You have to plan out your trips down the mountain, and I don't plan to head south until the day I leave. Driving those hills in and out is scary enough; I don't want to push my luck.

I stop at Trader Joe's to buy some essentials when I'm near the base of the mountain. I plan to get enough to last me the week.

I'm passing strangers while I mosey through each aisle, mainly on autopilot and dragging my feet. I'm starting to regret going alone, but I can't back out now. I'm thirty minutes away, and I'm too much of a cheap-ass to let that money go to waste. I'm on a teacher's salary, and we don't always get these opportunities of peace and solitude. Maybe I'll really enjoy myself. When was the last time I went anywhere alone?

Multiple bottles of wine jangle and clink together as I amble over to the cheese. I grab two blocks of Unexpected Cheddar and drop them into my cart. My eyes scan over the items I've collected so far, and I can't help but laugh.

It truly does look like I'm reverting back to my teenage years. I have so much junk in here, I guarantee I'll be breaking out in zits by day three. Thankfully, I brought a face mask.

My internal, humorous thoughts turn to gloom rather quickly. Gosh, I don't want to start over. I don't want to jump back into the dating scene. I don't want to tell my students when we return to the classroom in January that not only did I not get *the* ultimate gift, but I'm also single.

I wonder how long it'll take me to get over this. Two years is a long time with someone. I'm such an attentive, observant person. How did I not know Landon was ending things? I'm a teacher, planning out the year is my job. How did I not plan for *that*?

As I pass the cereal section, a cold chill creeps up my back, making the hairs on the nape of my neck rise. Like when you're alone, walking through a parking structure. Is someone hiding in one of the cars? Is someone watching you? It's a sixth sense; you can feel a pair of eyes on you, even if you can't see them.

It could be my imagination, but I get the feeling I'm being followed. I get these premonitions from time to time, and my gut reaction is typically spot on when it comes to sensing someone is invading my personal space.

When I turn around, I see a rather handsome gentleman tailing behind me, his cart too close to my heels.

He looks about my age, with dark hair, and over six feet tall.

His smile is friendly enough, but I retreat back to my cart so he doesn't think I'm inviting him into a conversation. People tend to be overly friendly at Trader Joe's, and today, I'm in no mood for pleasant chitchat.

I continue going through the aisles, grabbing whatever sounds appetizing, even if it won't get eaten. I'd rather have too much than too little.

When I'm in the frozen food section, that same niggling feeling plants its claws into my back as I grab a box of macaroni and cheese.

The same guy is right behind me, like he's my shadow. My arms tingle, and my grip tightens on the cart. We weave through the aisles, yet something about his movements sends a shiver down my spine. It's as if he's mirroring my every turn, a predator honing in on its prey. The air thickens with tension, and I can't shake the feeling that he's not just following; he's watching, waiting.

He offers the same smile a second time around, and this time, I muster up a tight-lipped grin that hopefully feels more forced than it looks. He reaches for the same box of macaroni, and I decide he must have zero sense of personal space.

"No egg nog?" he asks as he looks inside my cart. Christmas is in a few days, and I'm avoiding all the gingerbread or peppermint-flavored foods.

"I'm more of a wine gal," I respond, like it's not obvious by the multiple bottles in various shades of white, red, and rosé.

"I can see that. Not drinking alone, I take it? Or maybe that's preferable, in my case."

"And your case is?"

"Single for the holiday," he says.

Same, buddy.

"Ah, well, wish I could help you out, but I have a boyfriend." A sob wants to rip out of my chest, like a little critter fighting to escape a trap.

Single. Single. Single.

I begin to push my cart, assuming the conversation is over. That lie hurt more to say out loud than I expected, and the recovery of that confession has my nose turning red from the emotions fluttering inside me.

"Is that someone...Santa?" The guy is cute, but I am not in the mood for jokes—or a rebound, for that matter. And despite what my friends have been suggesting, I did not come on this trip with a mission of hooking up with a stranger.

"Funny," I muse and keep moving, grabbing a pack of cinnamon raisin bagels and dropping them in the cart.

"Are you from around here?" There he is again, right on my heels. This time, he finally does hit his cart in the back of my boots, and he has the grace to cringe when I bring accusing eyes his way.

Who actually asks where you're from in a grocery store?

"Or are you vacationing?" he tacks on.

"Neither," I bite out, frustration bubbling at the surface. "Just passing through."

"Ah, kind of like the snowstorm we are about to get," he murmurs, like he's yet another meteorologist my mom sent my way to persuade me *not* to go on this trip. Is this a setup? Did she track down some random Frosthaven Falls resident and hire him to try to scare me away from this?

Technically, the scariest part is driving up, and I haven't even left the grocery store to make that trek. The thought of slippery roads and snow add to my fear of making one wrong turn and driving off a cliff...which has happened before to visitors coming to ski. It's hard to shake the image of those vehicles disappearing into the void, a haunting reminder of how treacherous this journey can be when the roads aren't favorable.

"Luckily, I won't have to worry about that since I'm not going up the mountain." I walk over to checkout and the stranger follows behind me.

I've always been a wary person, and while this could be an overly friendly Good Samaritan, I don't have the energy for small talk with someone I'll never see again.

A Trader Joe's employee opens up a new register and calls him over.

Good. Now he can't talk to the back of my head. But now we're staring at each other while our groceries get bagged. The cashiers hand us our receipts simultaneously, and I accept mine with a grimace, already sensing he's going to trail behind me through the parking lot.

I tie my scarf tight around my neck, so tight it's practically a noose. The automatic doors open as a customer leaves, and a burst of frigid air blows at some stray hairs that didn't get pulled into my messy bun.

"After you," he offers and extends a hand when we try to exit at the same time.

"No, after you."

"Please, I insist."

"Can you just go?" I snap.

He picks up on the surly demand and doesn't fight me on the request. In fact, I scare him off completely.

I'm not exactly running back to my SUV, but I've picked up the zombie pace that was consuming me inside the grocery store. The depression dragging me down has been replaced with apprehension. I don't want this guy knowing which car I get into.

The wonky wheel attached to my cart squeaks in protest, fighting the sprinting pace and frozen ground as I finally reach my car.

Wow, it's getting cold.

I was prepared for the fifty-degree weather, but the wind chill is killing me.

As my body acclimates to the exterior temperature drop, the wind chill sweeps by and completely robs me of any warmth I was beginning to store.

I can already feel my lips turning blue. Why didn't I settle on Hawaii instead? Oh yeah, because that was wildly out of my budget.

Throwing the bags into my trunk, I return the cart and slam my door shut, but not before craning my head from left to right to see if a pair of eyeballs are watching me. The heat was on full blast when I parked, and it's a welcome relief when the seat warmer kicks in, too.

Looking at the empty passenger seat, I can't help but swallow a forming lump in my throat. Landon should be sitting there.

I was always the driver in our relationship. My passenger princess duties boiled down to giving horrible directions and getting carsick even in the front seat.

I'm one of those drivers who will always let you in when merging, as opposed to Landon, who liked to see how close we could get to crashing in a horrible accident before the other driver gave in.

My body does an involuntary spasm, so I shake loose the nostalgia and re-center myself.

"This trip is for you, Romee. To enjoy the break without the reminder of your ex, and to move on."

I'm not stupid. I know a two-year relationship won't magically be forgotten after a week's respite in the snow. But it can't hurt to try, right?

CHAPTER 3

DRIVING IN A
WINTER WONDERLAND

I've never driven in snow, and although I have all-wheel drive, I say a silent thank you when an ancient snow plow pulls in front of me.

"Jeez, can that thing even make it up the steep incline?" I follow closely behind him and grip my steering wheel. I feel a surge of gratitude as he carves a path through the snow, clearing the way for all of us daring enough to follow.

The roads are open for passage without chains on your tires, but they are recommended for those who have them. I do not have chains, so I'm lucky I can even accelerate on the roads without spinning in a three-sixty donut.

My phone bleats out an incoming call and I sigh.

My mom has awful timing, but I'm only driving ten miles per hour, so putting her fears to rest for the umpteenth time shouldn't be too distracting.

"Hi, Mom," I say when the car speaker beeps after connecting the call.

"Did you make it yet?"

"Nope, driving up now."

"Oh dammit, why did you answer my call? Focus on the road!"

"Because you would have freaked out if I didn't."

"True. Well, don't let me keep you. I want your full attention on driving, not on me."

"It's okay, I can chat for a minute. There's a huge snow plow in front of me preventing me from going eighty miles an hour."

"That's not funny." The utter fear in her voice makes me stifle a laugh.

"I'm kidding. I'm trying to get back to my old self, and that includes giving my mom a weekly heart attack."

"I understand, honey. I wish you didn't go. You could have flown out to see us."

"I'll be fine. It's a small town and not much happens here. I'll read, nap, maybe do some yoga. I think I need this more than anyone realizes, even if you disagree."

"You have Wi-Fi?"

"Yes, the cabin has Wi-Fi and a landline," I lie. I don't think there's a landline, and I immediately wish I could take it back, but then I'd really freak her out.

"Landon knows you went anyway? He had nothing to say about that?" my mom seethes.

"He knows and he doesn't care. He keeps proving that he was over the relationship a long time ago."

"I'm so sorry, sweetie."

"It's fi-fine." My voice breaks on the last word, my throat clogged with too many emotions I'm not ready to face. I can't cry on this call or she'll *really* worry about me, and I don't want that for her during this jolly time of year.

My mom was on the phone with me while I repacked my suitcase a second time prior to leaving. I sobbed as I removed the sexy lingerie I wouldn't be wearing and Landon's Christmas gift I'd inevitably return.

It was obvious she didn't want me going alone, but when I confessed the trip was still happening, she was supportive. She reminded me that I always make the best of a situation. She knows me inside and out, knows how *any* trip I'm going on is met with hesitation of what could go wrong. I have an eager need to be prepared, to expect anything, which is sometimes a weakness. Perhaps that's why the breakup hurt so bad. I truly wasn't prepared for it.

My mom always said I'm too cautious for my own good. I imagine the worst-case scenario all the time, and *apparently* it's not normal to think like that. I mean, she's completely right. I always end up having the best time on vacation, and this week alone would be no different.

I can hear her blasting Michael Bublé's Christmas album in the background, and I'm brought back to last Christmas when I brought Landon home with me. I'm sure she's dancing around the living room, swaying to the music, oblivious I'm replaying my last Christmas with Landon.

Releasing a forced cough so my voice appears normal, I add, "Tell Dad I miss you all, and I'll see you for my spring break."

"I will. Please keep in touch. I want my baby to be safe out there."

"The worst that will happen is I get a bit drunk and might text him."

"Delete his number now, Romee. Or do whatever those phones can do. Block your number or something."

"I'd block *his* number, Mom. But that only works if he texted me, and I don't think he'll be doing that."

Before we're able to continue the topic, the snow plow in front of me blares its horn.

"What is that? Romee, what was that?"

I have to ease on my brakes as I creep to a halt. Checking my rearview mirror to ensure the cars behind me don't cause an icy pileup, I'm relieved to see them stopping, too.

"Not sure," I tell her. "Looks like...oh Mom, deer! There's a deer in the middle of the road. How cool."

The snow plow releases three quick toots of his horn, scaring the deer and sending her darting into the thick woods surrounding us.

"Aww, she's gone," I say.

"Is there a lot of wildlife in Frosthaven Falls?"

"Polar bears and wolverines run rampant here, I heard."

My mom's silence is broken by quiet laughter on her end.

"I'm not *that* gullible, but that was funny," she admits.

"Hey, Mom, we're starting to go faster and the incline is less steep. I better let you go so I can focus. I think I'm closer than I realize."

"I love you. Text me all week. It won't bother me."

"Of course it won't," I tease, turning my wheel right at the fork in the road. "I'll talk to you soon, Mom. Love you, too."

I disconnect and lower the volume of the song I was listening to prior to the call.

21

My navigation informs me I'm a mile away, but it could take seven minutes to get there. I'd rather go slow and take my time anyway.

The main road reminds me a bit like Main Street at Disneyland, except barren and neglected. The vintage storefronts display neon open signs, but it's pretty deserted as I drive past.

I've seen photos and knew exactly what the town looked like, but I didn't expect such isolation when I turn down the dead end street to the cabin I'll be staying in.

A few houses are scattered among the blankets of snow, and I should have Googled this better. Had I known the nearest neighbor was *indeed* a mile away, I might have chosen a more expensive option.

But what does it matter? I thought I was coming here with Landon. Beggars can't be choosers.

When I spot the cabin to my right, I double-check the numbers in the address.

"Home sweet home."

CHAPTER 4

MARSHMALLOW WORLD

I turn off the car and gaze up at the cabin I'll be staying in for the next six nights.

There's nothing wrong with it, per se, but it looks...different.

Granted the listing no doubt emphasizes the best amenities and uses professional photos to highlight the views and whatnot, but it looks so old. Does this place really have Wi-Fi?

When I step out of my car, I grab my long coat from the backseat and drape myself in it. Good Lord, the chill up here is dreadful.

I take in the scenery. The house is backed up against an imposing hill, while the neighborhood itself sits precariously against a steep cliff. There's no garage, so I park in one of the two spaces assigned to the cabin.

23

I'm all alone out here, in more ways than one.

My breath is a bright white cloud that evaporates before me. Closing my eyes to take in the nature around me, I hear nothing. Absolutely nothing. But then, a burst of wind hits the empty air, rustling a nearby tree branch. The cabin has a strand of outdoor patio bulbs surrounding the roof, and they barely move in this wind, no doubt familiar with the disturbances up here and secured tight.

The air quality is noticeably different. There's no smog or pollution at this altitude, and the oxygen entering my lungs is as pure as the driven snow, so the saying goes. It's so crisp and wide open, the wind turbulence is powerful enough to shake my car.

"Merry Christmas, Rome—"

"Hi, there!"

Someone places their palm on my right shoulder as I spin around, ready to attack.

"Goodness gracious!" I shout, using the tone of voice set aside for the classroom when one of the kids sneaks up on me when I least expect it.

The older woman pulls her hand back like she got bit by an animal.

"Oh, I'm so sorry. I didn't mean to scare you."

"Well, you did." I check to see if she has a trail of footprints in the snow following behind her. "Did you appear out of thin air?"

"Sorry," she chuckles, not realizing she sent my blood pressure skyrocketing. "My husband always says I need a bell on me."

"Yeah, maybe a jingle bell. Those are in stock this time of year."

She doesn't laugh at my little joke, not even a lip twitch. Her strange behavior makes me wonder if I even saw her when I drove through. Where the hell did she come from?

I wait for her to introduce herself, but she just stares at me.

"You're a neighbor?" I begin, hoping she'll finish my sentence.

"Yes, you probably passed it on your way here, it's the first one. The big white mansion with the huge deck. That's mine."

She looks ultra smug and pleased with herself, like she is far superior to Linda, who has to rent out her house to strangers.

"Are you all alone?" Now it's her turn to ask what I'm doing here.

Crap.

"No, my boyfriend is, umm—" I try to think of a believable answer. I can't say he's meeting me here because it'll look odd if my car is the only one parked out front. I can't say he's already inside the house because I have no idea how long she's been watching me. A ripple

25

of fear hits me just as hard as that sudden wind. *Watching me.* Where did this lady come from?

"His friend is dropping him off. They went snowboarding together," I manage to say.

"Ah, I see. We got some great snow this year. Well, I'm up the road if you need anything. The big white mansion."

She repeats it again, like I forgot for a moment that she's the richest bitch in town.

She trudges back to her house, stepping in the same footprints she came in.

Why is she exercising in this weather? I'm sure she has acclimated to this climate, but who walks these streets for fun? And I say streets, but it's a narrow, dark road that doesn't have sidewalks. It's probably covered in black ice. And *do* bears live in these woods? I should Google that...

She's definitely used to this temperature, because while I'm layered up and wearing a full-length coat, she has a hoodie and jeans on. She's probably one of those people who considers this warm weather, and the second it hits fifty degrees, she turns the heat off. I plan on keeping the heat on all day and night, if I can help it.

Once the lady is out of view, I grab my suitcase and the groceries from the trunk. The cabin is elevated on a slope, so I have to slog up some stairs before I even get to the house itself. It only takes two trips up until everything is at the entrance.

A simple peephole is watching me as I press the unique six-digit code to get into the house: one-two-two-three-three-three. When the green light blinks, I open the front door and brace myself for more solitude.

Stomping my feet on the welcome mat so I don't track in dirt and snow, I wait for the musty odor of a sealed-up house to infiltrate my nose.

Instead, I'm pleasantly surprised by the fresh pine aroma lingering in the air. That could be nature, for all I know. Trees surround the charming little cabin that already gives off that clean, crisp fir scent.

The downstairs is small, with a cozy living room and fireplace, full kitchen and dining room, bathroom with a sink and toilet only, a hall closet, and a little corner mudroom where you can hang your coat and take your boots off.

When I reach the master bedroom on the second floor, I accidentally swing the door open so hard it crashes into the wall. It has a smooth hinge that I wasn't prepared for when I opened it.

"Shit!" I check behind the door and see a little dent in the drywall–probably the lock head smashing into the wall. I wipe at it for no reason other than to assess the damage. There's a small security deposit that I'll get back,

27

assuming I don't burn the place down—or keep knocking dents in the walls.

It'll be fine, and I doubt anyone would notice anyway. It's behind a door. I can't be the first person to misjudge the tension.

When I drop my weekender bag on the bed, I see someone has left two candy canes in the shape of a heart on each pillow.

"Oh, God," I moan, angrily wiping at the welling tears.

I'm not in full-on Grinch mode, but I don't need the reminder I'll be sleeping in this bed alone. Swiping at the four candy canes, I crush them in my hands until they snap like pencils, then toss them in the trash.

CHAPTER 5

CHESTNUTS ROASTING ON AN OPEN FIRE

W hen I'm done unpacking my groceries, I get to work.

I'm not generally a paranoid person, but years of watching true crime documentaries and the fact that I'm alone has led me to take necessary precautions.

Are hidden cameras in an Airbnb illegal? Surely. Linda might seem like a sweet, old woman, but you never know. She might have a voyeur fetish and a collection of sexual escapades over the years from unassuming guests. Granted, I'm alone and won't be performing any of those acts, thank you very much, but I still don't want someone spying on me while I eat my weight in junk food and undoubtedly cry myself to sleep each night.

Juggling a wine glass in one hand and cell phone in the other, I open the camera and scan the room, waiting for an obnoxious red dot to become more apparent in my lens.

I save time and skip the bedrooms I won't be using, instead focusing on the main living area and kitchen on the first floor and the areas upstairs.

So far, nothing is jumping out at me. I check the usual places where hidden cameras are placed: smoke detectors and electronics. Most don't need Wi-Fi, and unless it's hooked up to a USB that saves the footage to be retrieved at a later date, I don't see anything unusual. I'll check again once it's dark. I'm like Santa right now, making a list and checking it twice. I'd rather be safe than sorry.

The next thing I do is wipe down all the surfaces with a Clorox wipe. The previous guests could have been complete slobs, and who knows how lazy the cleaning crew might have been. For extra measure, I run the dishwasher with the essential items I'll be using all week: a place setting for one—kill me!—complete with a bowl, plate, mug, drinking glass, knife, spoon, fork, and a few other common cooking items.

The sky is getting darker by the minute, and delicate snowflakes are dropping at an increasingly steady rate. It looks rather peaceful, if not a little ominous.

I'm on the second floor, which has a great room overlooking the front of the house. It's like a mini family room, complete with a couch, chaise lounge, and old bookshelf. There are no blinds or curtains up here, because you get an unobstructed view of the Western Hemisphere. Thanks to it being elevated from the main road, the gorgeous panoramic view of the trees and snowy sky are breathtaking.

A glance outside makes me realize how dark it is. Walking over to the largest window and placing my cheek against it, I realize I can't even see any signs of civilization, not even the telltale glow of the nosy neighbor's Big White Mansion. They don't have street lights out here, and the neighbor's footprints from earlier have disappeared.

I decide to make myself some dinner, so I head back to the first floor and toss my macaroni in the microwave. The giant fireplace is calling to me, so I grab some small logs and place them inside. Linda has a huge collection of pre-split wood, for which I'm grateful. I brought a few Duraflame logs to jumpstart the fire since I'm not the most outdoorsy gal. I'm also too lazy to prepare kindling and all that, so I surround the little log with large pieces that will all catch quicker thanks to the hassle-free Duraflame.

The microwave timer dings at me to signal the food is ready, so I grab my freshly cleaned bowl and choose the comfiest looking leather seat in the family room. The fire is already warming up the drafty old house.

When I turn to a nearby window, I'm struck down with a frisson of dread.

The blinds are pointed down.

I rectify that immediately by twisting the pole and pointing the blinds facing up. Do people not realize you can see inside someone's house if the lights are on? I don't care if I'm the only person in a mile radius or not.

I scan the room and realize *all* the blinds are like this.

It takes me a minute to fix every window on the first floor, but I feel a thousand percent better after.

I'm all alone out here, and the last thing I need is some neighbor stopping by, peeping through the windows and finding out my boyfriend is in fact *not* here with me. Could that happen? Maybe. Will it happen? Probably not.

Finally able to relax with my food, I turn on the TV, well prepared to eat this two-serving meal in one sitting.

CHAPTER 6

ON A SNOWY CHRISTMAS EVE, EVE NIGHT

The sound machine I brought with me was a lifesaver. I didn't realize how *quiet* nature can be until I was in the middle of nowhere. No neighbors. No random car doors slamming in the middle of the night. No kids staying up past their bedtime and racing in the streets.

I can't sleep in the quiet. I need some type of white noise to distract my racing thoughts.

And today, waking up to a new morning, I'm going to see how long I go without texting Landon.

When he broke up with me, there was that week of neutrality when we were coordinating returning each other's things and other logistics. We weren't on never-speaking-again terms, but now we are. It's been a week since he broke my heart, and I'm still fighting my brain about texting him one more time.

"Romee, I'm not in love with you anymore. I don't think we were meant to be together."

I straighten my slouched back and try to find my backbone.

I survived my first night here alone. I can live without the man I thought I'd be with forever. It's a new day, and I am a new woman.

I hop down the stairs, refreshed and energized, in total denial that there is an emotional breakdown coming.

It's after nine o'clock. I haven't slept this late in so long. My body seems to have permanently adjusted to a six a.m. wakeup call, since I have to be ready and out the door an hour after if I want to get to my classroom on time.

The elementary school I teach at is less than a mile away from my apartment back in the city, a lucky break when I applied there four years ago.

All my fifth-grade kiddos were so excited for me to go on this trip. I've grown close to the families of our small private school, and it's going to kill me when I return and they inquire about "our" trip.

I exhale and grab the cup I left out last night. Think of something else. *Anything* else.

The mug I've chosen for the week is a yellow, vintage-looking thing with a crackle glaze that could probably sell in an Anthropologie store for fifteen dollars a pop. It's rustic and cheerful, and even though yellow reminds me of egg yolks, I need a happy color right now.

Linda stocked her kitchen with Nespresso pods, so I pop one in and grab the half-and-half I got at the grocery store.

What shall I do today?

Let's do a weather check.

Grabbing the cord to the blinds above the kitchen sink, I yank them up and am met with a wall of white.

I better not be snowed in.

Strolling to the front door with my steaming mug of coffee, I squint one eye through the peephole, bracing myself to ensure I'm not about to be ambushed by a group of enthusiastic Christmas carolers.

I'm being ridiculous. It was ten degrees last night and there's not a footprint to be seen in the vast expanse of fluffy snow.

But I can't help it. I check a second time and feel satisfied.

I crack open the door, but a gust of wind snatches the handle from my hand and it flies open, bringing a shimmering cascade of snow with it. The shock of cold freezes me for a moment, but when I feel the fleeting chill of snowflakes melting on my socks, I spring into action and slam the door shut.

"Damn!" Mother Nature is a powerful beast. Ugh, wet socks are the worst.

I'm not tempting fate and leaving the cabin today, not in this condition. Looks like I'd blow away if I even got to my car in one piece. Knowing me, I'd slip and fall down the stairs, break an ankle or get a concussion, and the cleaning team would find me next week. My mom would be so mad.

Maybe the sun will decide to stop hiding behind those heavy looking clouds in a few hours and I can go out for a walk.

But what if I run into that nosy neighbor? *Was* she even a neighbor? She claimed to own the mansion, but she could just as easily be a criminal who waits for these vacation rentals to be empty so they can pillage and squat in the warm house until they hit their next mark.

I can't be stuck inside all week. It's Saturday and two days before the big day.

Christmas falling on a Monday should be illegal, but I don't make the rules. And I didn't have the best options for dates, so I'll be checking out Thursday—if I last that long.

There's nothing forcing me to stay the entire time. Maybe I'll be here for two nights and realize I miss my bed. I can leave the day before Christmas and spend the rest of my break sobbing into the pillow that still smells like Landon.

I'm standing in the small foyer when it happens.

A floorboard directly above me releases a groan, like someone applied half their weight, realized their mistake, and returned to their hiding spot. The heart-wrenching, punch in the gut reaction consumes me like an exorcism.

Part of me wants to pretend I didn't hear it at all. I already searched the whole house, and I found nothing. No one. I haven't even left, so it's not like someone could sneak in while I was out.

The other part of me—the rational side—knows this is an old house, and old houses make noise. Maybe it wasn't a floorboard. Maybe it was the wind blowing at the window frame. It *did* just bang the door open.

My fingertips are going numb, the first sign I'm starting to catastrophize.

"Stop, Romee," I tell myself. "It's an old house. It's a windy day."

When I say this, another gust of wind wraps around the house with an audible keening, as if saying, "See, it's just the wind."

I 'll be wired for days if I allow myself more than three cups of coffee, so after a blueberry scone and a banana, I hand wash the dishes, including the yellow mug so it doesn't tempt me to make another cup, and leave them drying on the rack.

My trusty Stanley gets replenished with fresh ice water, and once I have a new pair of dry socks, I add another log to the fire.

I glance near the front door, like I'm expecting someone to knock.

Shoot, did I lock it?

When I walk to the entrance, I step into another small puddle of melted snow.

"Oh, you've got to be kidding me," I huff, peeling off my second pair of socks and wishing I brought more. At this rate, I'll have no clean pairs by Christmas Day.

I wipe up the puddle of water and blow some stray hairs out of my face.

The deadbolt is secure, so I run upstairs, grab yet *another* pair of socks—and slippers, while I'm at it—and hang my two pairs of wet socks on little hooks I found on the mantle that are no doubt meant for Christmas stockings. Then I plop myself in that large leather chair with a cozy blanket.

Netflix is lit up on the TV above the fire, advertising Christmas movie after cheesy Christmas movie. The last thing I need is some corny Hallmark story about an unlikely couple who fall in love on the first date. I need the literal opposite.

I turn on where I left off in *Stranger Things* and settle in for an intense, creepy day filled with gore and blood.

CHAPTER 7

OH CHRISTMAS TREE, OH CHRISTMAS TREE

A fter four episodes, I fell asleep in the chair.

I was out for maybe an hour and was pleased to see the bright glow of sunshine in the room. The snow has momentarily stopped, and I see blue skies out the window.

Opening the front door again to gauge how much snow has melted, I'm ecstatic to see my car without a huge white backpack of snow on the roof.

When I turn to go back in, a pathetic looking tree I hadn't noticed before is dripping with moisture. A branch blows in the breeze like he's waving at me.

It's a sad little thing, with broken branches and lopsided empty spaces. A Charlie Brown tree, if I ever saw one. I think it's a balsam. It sure *looks* like a Christmas tree. It could be an oak or birch for all I know, but it has pointy ends and smells heavenly.

40

"Damn you," I say to it. "You're the ugliest Christmas tree I've ever seen. But you can't be alone out here, too."

The only reason I'm giving this any consideration is because there's a wall of tools along the back side of the house. Linda was smart to keep it out of sight, because I'm certain the occupants using this cabin would be put off if the first thing they noticed was a wall of torture devices as seen in *The Texas Chainsaw Massacre*. Saws, pruners, and sheers ranging from handheld to massive line the wall near my little tree. Granted, they're used for chopping wood, but still.

"If I bring you inside, promise you won't make a huge mess?"

A few water drops make a loud *plunk* on the heavy wood beams, and I add, "You're lucky you're three feet tall."

It doesn't take much to saw the damp tree stump. It'll have to dry out before I can decorate it.

Hold on, decorate it? Where is this coming from?

I did pass a country store at the top of the mountain right before turning into the residential streets. They have to have something festive in there. Plus, I need to get out of here and stretch my legs.

Taking the small tree through the back door isn't as challenging as I was expecting. I let it dry out near the fireplace. Not too close a branch might fall in and burn the house down, but close enough the heat and dry environment will soak up some of the moisture.

I bundle myself up with multiple layers, close the front door behind me, and key in the code to lock it up.

The icy stairs down to my car almost get the better of me, but luckily the bannister helps me make it safely to the ground.

I have to sit in my car for a whole five minutes while the heat turns on and defrosts the windows. I'm bouncing in the driver seat, waiting for my seat to warm up, too.

"Hurry, hurry, I'm freeeeezing."

When the engine is no longer a block of ice, I put the car in reverse and expect to slide right off the embankment. But my wheels grip the ground, and I'm able to back out and head toward town.

I drive five miles per hour, white-knuckling the steering wheel and leaning dangerously close to the airbag so I can see.

Right when I pull into a parking spot for the store, my phone rings. Please, not my mom.

I look at my phone screen with fingers crossed.

Luckily, it's my best friend from work, Emily. She was in the minority of our friend group and was on Team "Please Don't Go Alone."

"Hey, Em. How are you?"

"Hi, love! Checking in to see how things are going. How was the first night?"

"Fine, nothing too crazy to report," I say with more cheer than I feel.

"So, you're still there?"

"Yes, why do you ask?"

"Some of us at school have a pool going. To see how long you'll actually last."

"What? Are you serious?"

"Romee, you're alone, in a huge old cabin, in the middle of nowhere. And on Christmas!"

"So?"

"Isn't it creepy? I can't even watch a scary movie by myself. And you're sleeping there for the week?"

"It's really not that bad. It's so quiet. It's kind of nice. I watched *Stranger Things* and finished a whole bottle of wine last night."

"On top of being alone, you watched a scary show? I say this with love: Did Landon's betrayal mess with your judgment?"

"Emmmmm," I whine, like I'm one of her kindergartners.

"Sorry, Romee. It's my segue to see how you're doing."

"I'm okay. I'll get over this...in about five years."

"You are a strong woman. The strongest I know. Give yourself time to grieve, and you'll be back to your normal self before you know it."

"It's easier being up here, knowing he probably isn't thinking about me anyway."

"Does he know you went alone?"

"Yes, I told him the last time we spoke in person. He probably thinks I'm crazy, too."

"Maybe you need to find yourself a hot, bearded lumberjack to rebound with."

"I *am* going into the store now, so I'll keep my eyes peeled," I say with sarcasm. I came here to be alone, and I intend to keep it that way.

"If you want to FaceTime me while I wrap Christmas gifts, maybe we can start a movie together and sync it up."

"That honestly sounds amazing, Em. I'll text you later, 'kay?"

"Love you. Merry Christmas Eve Eve."

I disconnect the call and step out of my car, then slip my wireless earbuds in to deter conversation.

Why is it so frowned upon for a woman to travel alone? As if I can't take care of myself? There's this strange stigma I never even realized existed, as if the world is a minefield just waiting to ensnare me. Why is it assumed that women traveling solo are in constant danger?

I make brief eye contact with the person behind the register in this cramped little store. She and I exchange quick smiles as I browse. Everything is wildly expensive, probably due to both the tourist population and the cost of transportation this high up.

But I do find a strand of tinsel and white lights. Normally, I am anti-tinsel. It's messy and looks cheap, but that's all they have, and I can't be picky. It is, after all, less than forty-eight hours before Christmas Day. And instead of ornaments, I find a bag of ten jingle bells I can hang on the branches and a pack of candy canes.

"Did you find everything you needed, darling?" the sales lady asks, with a twinge of a Southern accent. Her cherubic face has pink blotches on her rounded cheeks.

"Yes, thank you so much."

She rings me up, and I hand over the cash I brought.

"Here, a little something for ya from Mrs. Claus," she whispers with a wink.

She adds a frosted snowman cookie on display wrapped in cellophane.

"Thank you, that's so sweet."

"Are you in one of the rentals?" she asks.

"Yes, my boyfriend and I are. He's waiting for me."

"Oh, well, we can't forget about him." She adds another cookie to the bag. "Merry Christmas! You stay safe."

As the motion-sensored doors open for me, I turn around and see her whispering something in her coworker's ear. She watches me, immediately stopping her conversation with a smile and another wave. Except this time, she doesn't look as cheerful as she did ten seconds ago.

I wave back with a half-hearted smile and a semi-limp hand.

There haven't been too many crimes in Frosthaven Falls—I would know; I looked up articles before coming here. While there have been a few people who have "fallen off the face of the earth" and gone missing, that's to be expected in any city. More concerning are the fatal accidents involving visitors who drove off the cliffs, often attributed to a combination of reckless behavior and the treacherous conditions. The steep, winding roads can easily catch an unsuspecting driver off guard, especially when the weather turns icy. It's chilling to think that one moment of distraction or a miscalculated turn could lead to a deadly plunge. But nothing else screams unusual; just the risks that come with the allure of a town perched high in the sky."

"Gosh, Romee. Knock it off." I set the bag on the passenger seat, annoyed with myself for assuming the worst yet again.

Rolling up the sleeves of the herringbone coat I bought specifically for this trip, I take a deep breath and try to shake off the uneasy feeling poisoning my veins. I had imagined wearing this coat while Landon proposed on the balcony, as we sipped hot toddies and kissed under falling snow and mistletoe.

I wonder what he's doing for Christmas? Landon's parents live on the East Coast, so I doubt he'll take an expensive, last-minute flight out. He gave me no input on what he'd be doing for the approved time off he requested prior to our breakup.

When I turn on my car, Thurl Ravenscroft's distinctive voice sings from the radio.

"Your heart is full of unwashed socks, your soul is full of gunk, Mr. Grinch!"

MY SOCKS.

I left my socks above the fireplace. I need to get back as soon as possible to make sure I haven't set the cabin on fire.

It takes me just as long to drive back as it did leaving. When I near the house, I decrease my speed and press the brakes, but my car starts to drift on a patch of ice and I'm headed right for the stone retaining wall that butts up against the hill.

"Shit...shit...shit!"

My car finally stops about a millimeter from the wall, and I sag back in the seat in relief. I gaze up at the house and am happy not to see a gaping hole of raging flames out the roof.

Stomping up the steps to get rid of any dirt and slush on my boots, I wait at the door and put in the code.

When it beeps to unlock, I unwind my scarf and remove my beanie.

Wiping my feet one last time on the welcome mat before I enter, I'm surprised when I'm met with another huge puddle of water when I step inside.

CHAPTER 8

CAROL OF THE BELLS

H uh. I swear I wiped up the mess from earlier, the one that soaked my socks.

I rewind the action in my head and can't be sure I got it all. And I can't be certain some snow didn't blow in when I left for the store, either.

Regardless, I walk to the kitchen, set the items on the counter, and grab a large serrated bread knife.

What's the harm in checking the house one more time?

When I am certain the downstairs is empty, I grab a towel and wipe up the mess.

Holding the knife in one hand and my shopping bag in the other, I carefully remove the jingle bells.

Instead of keeping them inside the house, I place them on the outside door handle. That way, if someone is in the house and they try to leave out the front while I'm upstairs, I'll hear the jingling the second it swings open.

Obviously, I hope nothing comes of this, but at least I'll know I'm being paranoid and some Frosthaven Falls residents aren't out to get me.

Tiptoeing up the stairs, I clench the knife so hard I could probably stab my way through concrete. I should have grabbed another weapon for my left hand, but I already feel my fingers tingling with unease.

The first room I inspect is clear. It's difficult to open the loud closet doors without shaking the upper half of the house and giving a heads up I'm waiting to catch someone spying on me, but I'm able to confirm the two spare bedrooms are empty.

I don't find anything creepy like a sleeping bag and protein bar wrappers.

Last is my room, and as I push open the door, it bangs against the wall again.

"Shit," I hiss under my breath. This time, I left a huge dent in the drywall. The hinges are too clean and could use some dirt or dust to cut back on the ease of the opening. Hopefully no one notices that when I leave.

My eyes scan the room for any signs of disturbance, but it appears just as I left it. My bed hasn't magically been slept in after I made it this morning, and as far as I know, none of the clothes in my suitcase have been ransacked.

But did I shut the bedroom door when I left the house? I've been trying to keep it open due to the stupid hole in the wall, but I can't be certain I didn't close it from habit.

It's not a huge red flag, so I dismiss it and accept the less threatening truth that I probably let some snow in as I left for the store. Big deal. I need to stop acting like someone is trying to break in. I'm in the middle of nowhere and don't have anyone around for miles.

Okay, miles might be a stretch, but it works in this scenario.

"I need a drink," I say to no one, since I am certain I'm the only weirdo in this house.

Walking down the stairs, I grab the jingle bells that never made a sound and prep my little tree for some love.

The fire has died out, which I should have noticed earlier since the living room wasn't a sauna when I walked through. The heat functions well in the house—surprising, given how outdated it is—but the fire truly adds that extra layer of warmth and coziness. I add a few more logs to keep it blazing bright.

I'm even getting better at starting the fire without the help of the Duraflame. Look at me! I'm not as helpless as I thought.

My ugly little tree is still damp, but way better than it was outside. I wrap it in tinsel and lights while juggling my glass of white wine, then add the bells in a chaotic pattern.

There's only enough for the front of the tree, so I look to the nearby corner of the room and decide it'll be happy over there.

It's not going to win any awards, but it'll do. I add some candy canes as well.

I realize it's missing a star, so I saunter off to the kitchen with my empty glass of wine, refill it, fish the cork out of the trash, and stab it in the center with an ice pick from the utensil drawer.

The branch sticking out at the top isn't very thick, but I have to shove that cork in to make it fit.

"Perfect."

I admire it with slightly intoxicated vision and then burst into tears.

CHAPTER 9

CHRISTMAS TREE FARM

"**H**ow long did you let yourself cry?" Emily asks over our FaceTime call.

"An hour," I sniffle. "Maybe more. I lost count." My face is still swollen and puffy, the whites of my eyes a solid pink. I keep it to myself that I cried for almost two hours straight while chugging another bottle of wine and listening to sad music.

"I should have come with you! Oliver would have forgiven me."

"No way. It's your first Christmas as husband and wife."

"But my bestie needs me."

Suddenly, Oliver's face appears on the FaceTime screen.

"I could have gone with you lovely ladies. I don't mind being the third wheel," he interrupts.

"Gosh, why did you have to marry someone so sweet, Em? He's perfect."

Tears are pooling in the corners of my eyes, and I take a gulp of wine to pretend I'm not about to break out into a blubbering mess.

"He snores. He's not perfect, trust me," she says in a hushed voice.

"And your bestie over here has no idea what a Christmas budget means." Oliver playfully nudges her shoulder, and I want to puke.

"I might have drunk texted Landon," I admit.

"Oh, Romee." Emily has politely shoved Oliver out of the way so it's back to just us girls. I love Oliver, but he doesn't need to see me wallowing like this.

"This is what I said: 'I miss you. I wish you were here with me.'"

Emily doesn't say a word, but instead, bites her bottom lip with downcast eyes.

"It's fine. Landon didn't even reply. I think I would have preferred him to say something passive-aggressive like: 'We broke up, remember?' His silence hurts worse, like he can't be bothered to respond. What do you think he's doing? Hang on, I need more wine."

I leave my phone propped up on some books as I shuffle to the kitchen for a refill. *Home Alone* is playing in the background on both our TVs. "Rocking Around the Christmas Tree" is blaring, and I'm losing my buzz.

"Bless you," Emily says when I return.

"I didn't sneeze," I inform her.

"What? I could have sworn I heard a sneeze."

A strange wave of panic ripples against my limbs, fear blossoming in my chest like a flower. The wine in my glass pulsates in my shaking hand.

"You heard a sneeze on my end of the phone?" I confirm.

"Yes, I swear. I don't think it was the movie."

We synchronized it at the same time, so if she heard a sneeze in the movie on my end, she would have heard it on her side, too.

"This is freaking me out." Emily rubs her arms, that same element of fear hitting her a hundred miles away.

"Maybe it was the house. I didn't hear anything."

"You didn't? Romee..."

"I mean, I'm a little drunk, so I can't be certain."

"This is too weird. I mean, I'm also buzzed. Look how I just wrapped this hideous thing."

She presents me with a lopsided, lumpy package covered in red paper with gold polka dots.

"Hey, it's the thought that counts, right?" I laugh. "I should tell you what happened earlier." I take a big sip of wine right as Emily does the same.

"Do I want to know?"

"It's nothing, I promise. But it's almost as if someone was in the house and didn't clean up the melted snow at the front door."

"Romee, come home now!" she shouts at me. She's holding her phone with the camera focused on her mouth. "I'm serious. Leave!"

"Even if I wanted to, I can't. It's snowing, and I can't drive at night like this. I'd have to wait for tomorrow when the snow melts."

"This is ridiculous. You checked the house?"

"Several times since I've been here."

"I'm not surprised. Did you bring your mace?"

"It's actually in my car. I should go down and get it."

"And risk the freezing temperatures? Get it tomorrow and sleep with a knife."

"A knife?" I shriek.

"Want me to call you instead and we can stay on speakerphone all night? That way, if anything happens, I can hear you?"

"Nothing is going to happen to me here, but I appreciate your concern."

"I don't like this, Rome."

Emily is looking into the iPhone camera, peering behind me.

"Is that a Christmas tree I see?"

56

I grab the phone and flip the lens around so it shows my measly tree.

"Oh, that thing? Yep, cut him down myself. Isn't he cute?"

"I didn't think you were celebrating. Look at you cutting down your own tree like you own a Christmas tree farm."

We're both quiet for a moment, and Emily adds, "I wish I was there wrapping my presents with you. Are you doing okay, for real?"

"Honestly, Em, I don't know. I didn't see it coming. And I'm prepared for everything. You know that. But I wasn't expecting this. How did I not know?"

"You won't be alone forever."

I know her intentions are sweet, but I can't help but hear a warning in that sentence. Typical me, trying to find the ominous in the innocent.

"I'll be okay, I promise," I confess. "Come on, let's keep watching the movie."

When Kevin McCallister has been reunited with his family, it's close to nine o'clock, and the wine is making me oh so tired. I blow Emily a few kisses and we say goodbye.

I also promise to text her when I'm in bed for the night and again tomorrow when I wake up. It'll be Christmas Eve, after all.

The fire has almost died, and the room is dimming by the minute. I grab the two socks that are almost stiff from hanging on the hooks all day.

Wait—didn't I have two pairs, four socks total?

I drop them to the floor, not only because I'm beginning to panic all over again, but because they are scorching hot.

Crouching on my hands and knees, I lower my face into the dying flames and search the ash and glowing coals.

Did two socks fall in? They might have. I honestly forgot all about them after the whole water puddle fiasco. It could have happened while I was gone, when I put on more logs, or two minutes ago.

Am I in danger? How many times have I searched the house and come back with nothing? All the strange things happening could have been complete accidents—or mishaps due to my ineptitude and daily inebriation.

But my perception of a threat is heightened, either way.

To clear my mind, I return to the kitchen with my empty wine glass and clean up my mess from dinner.

I might need to implement this one serving dishware rule at my apartment. It's so easy when you only use one spoon or one bowl. Easy clean up. And I will be a party of one for the foreseeable future.

My clean wine glass lies next to the blue mug on the drying rack, and I walk back to the dimming living room.

I almost don't take notice due to the lack of light, but it sticks out like a sore thumb.

One of the windows in the main living area has blinds that are tilted down.

CHAPTER 10

BLUE CHRISTMAS

A nervous laugh escapes my lips, and I purse them inward until they are pinched closed.

Running to the window, I grab the little pole and twirl it through my fingers, just in case someone is on the other side looking inward.

It's a quick motion that leaves me little time to investigate outside, but maybe my problem is actually coming from inside the house.

"You forgot this blind on the first day," I whisper to myself, trying to calm my escalating heart rate.

But it's too late. Every worst case scenario runs like a film reel in my head.

Someone is hiding in the house.

Someone is here to kill me.

But then I look at my little Christmas tree and see the cork for a star.

I've had a lot of wine these past two days—more than I've had in a while. It could have been an accident when I looked out the window and tilted them differently. My habitual practices might have taken a back seat due to my sloppy brain.

But as Emily suggested, I sleep with a knife in my bed anyway.

And when I wake up in the morning, I think I might go home. I'm sick of being by myself but not truly feeling alone.

Mother Nature has other plans on the morning of Christmas Eve.

It's so dark out, I have to double check the time to make sure it's not midnight.

A white-gray haze replaces the blue sky I saw yesterday, bringing with it a measure of foreboding.

My feet are wrapped in slippers as I add a crew neck sweatshirt over my pajamas. Even with the heater going all night, standing so close to the window sends a flurry of ice up my spine.

"Better make a fire."

I walk down the stairs, knife still in hand, waiting for the next surprise to put me in cardiac arrest.

But everything is quiet—the scary quiet I was met with my first night here.

I sift through the ashes for any sign of fabric or strings. The metal poker combs through the bits of wood that didn't burn all the way, and I can't really tell either way if my socks are somewhere in there.

To extinguish that delusion, I add more logs and move on.

All simple accidents, nothing more.

Walking to the drying rack, I grab my yellow mug and add some hot coffee to it.

The bulbs gleaming outside are the only light coming from the exterior. I flip various switches in the kitchen hoping I come across the one that controls their usage.

"Ugh, turn off!"

None of the flipped switches are alleviating the eerie glow outside. Linda had to have splurged on those heavy duty lights. They withstand rain, snow, and wind.

"Fine," I begin, cupping the hot mug and walking to my favorite chair. "It's not like I have to pay the utility bill while I'm here."

My weather app is open, and I scroll to the left and see nothing but snow-flurried clouds for the next twenty-four hours.

"I'm stuck here," I admit to my little tree. "I think I'll call you Marv."

It's an ode to my favorite Wet Bandit from *Home Alone*.

"You're probably going to die soon."

I realize after it's said just how morbid it sounded. Like a weird omen, when I was merely trying to point out how I didn't even put the small base of his trunk in water. The store didn't have Christmas tree stands, but he seems to be doing fine propped up in the corner.

"I'm gonna go make breakfast."

The isolation has turned me into Tom Hanks with his volleyball. But it's better to talk to Marv than to fight the urge to text Landon.

I grab my phone and see our last text exchange, the one where he actually responded, prior to my drunken shenanigans. We were confirming where we'd meet so we could exchange all the items we left at each other's places.

I thought about holding out on a couple of key things he needed, like his second pair of gym shoes. Then I could text him a day or two before I was set to leave and say, "Oh, wow, look what I found. We better meet up so I can give them back."

Then maybe he'd see me, realize us being apart wasn't good for him, and he'd ask for a second chance. My blue Christmas would be gold and shiny again!

Instead, I kept his college sweatshirt like it belonged to me. I didn't have the heart to give it back. It doesn't even smell like him anymore because I've worn it so many times.

Berkeley is printed in chunky square lettering across my chest.

Hugging myself tight like I would if Landon was in front of me, I set a timer for thirty minutes.

That's all the time I get today to cry. No more.

When the tears have dried up after my allotted time, I spend the rest of the afternoon reading.

And when I'm not doing that, I'm watching and waiting for the sky to tear open and reveal slivers of blue. But I don't see that happening anytime soon.

The domestic thriller I finished was decent. I'm sick of the alcoholic, unreliable narrator, but it was a good distraction. I feel like I never have enough time to read, and I make it a goal to read more books in my free time. I'm going to have lots of that going forward.

I release a whiny, exaggerated cry.

"Just kidding, Marv. I'm trying to move on. I'll shut up now."

Looking at my little tree, I can't help but feel at ease with all it symbolizes. A new year is coming, and it'll be a good chance for me to start over.

"Shall I take a long, hot bath, Marv?"

A loud pop from the fireplace makes me jump. It's large enough to resemble a firework burst. It startles me hard enough that my blood starts pumping overtime.

Another intense burst crackles as the flames find pockets of moisture in the dried out logs. I used to love the sound of a rip-roaring fire, but now the unpredictability is another jump scare I don't need, especially since my radar is on high alert after that damn book and the weird stuff that's been going on.

I walk to the main window that overlooks the front and tug the blinds up, hoping for a different view.

But as expected, the snow hasn't let up.

It looks like someone left a streak of whitish gray paint on the glass, covering my view and the miles before me in a ghostly, apocalyptic world. I'm basically all alone up here, and I can't leave even if I wanted to.

I slip on my boots, still wearing my pajamas and Landon's sweatshirt, and walk out the front door.

The air has a thick, fog-like quality, bringing with it an acute arctic blast. I immediately see my breath when I breathe out and wrap my arms around me, which does absolutely nothing. Oh my God! Are my nose hairs freezing? Never in my life did I imagine *that* happening.

I peer over the railing down to my car. The snow level has reached the tops of my tires, and even if I trusted myself to drive in this weather, I can barely see fifty feet in front of me, and I'm not even sure my tires would get any traction backing out of my parking spot.

"Dammit."

I slowly shake my head in disapproval, pissed at myself for coming here in the first place. What did I expect? I'd have a mid-life epiphany out here? I'd get over Landon and have the time of my life? This is ridiculous. I'm almost out of wine–three bottles was never going to be enough–and I truly feel like I'm losing my mind. Today me is very unhappy with the me who made decisions at Trader Joe's.

"Get over it, Rome. Wait for the snow to stop, then get out of here." I hug myself tighter, prepared to go inside.

As I turn to head back, my eye catches the spot where Marv was once rooted. I practically run to the location because I'm hoping it's just my imagination.

66

The snow should have covered any signs of life, so when I'm standing directly above what caught my eye, I can't deny its existence.

A fresh footprint is in the snow right outside the cabin.

I set my foot delicately inside the shape as my body is flooded with fear.

My boot has plenty of space at the toe area as my heel connects to the back. This is a footprint much larger than mine. A man's, most likely.

My chaotic brain filters through justifiable excuses as to why someone, anyone, would have a reason to be on the property. To get *this close* to the front door.

The wind blows some trees, causing me to swivel to my left. I'm half expecting to see a man with an ax—or worse, a chainsaw—raised above his head, ready to split me in two. But there's nothing. There's no one.

I'm surrounded by white clouds coming out in thick puffs as I exhale deeply, on the verge of hyperventilating when I acknowledge what's right in front of me. It's not only the footprint in the snow that consumes me with fear.

From the angle I'm at, facing the cabin from this spot where the footprint is, it's right by the window that had the blinds facing down. This position is a perfect spot to see inside and watch me.

My brain begins prioritizing all the necessary functions to survive.

Breathe, Romee, breathe.
Inhale, exhale, ignore the buzzing in your ear caused by
the panic trying to consume you.
Breathe.
And get the hell out of here.

CHAPTER 11

LET IT SNOW

I sprint to the door, nearly slipping and falling on my ass in the process. My movements are frantic and messy, and I grab onto the door frame as I ensure I'm safely inside. I slam the door behind me and fumble with the lock like someone is actually chasing me.

Police. Call the police.

The fire has grown in size, and I don't even notice the snap, crackle, and pops as I locate my phone and dial.

A dispatcher answers immediately.

"Nine-one-one, this is Frosthaven Falls dispatch, what is your emergency?"

"Hi, my name is Romee Anderson. I'm staying in an Airbnb rental, and I think I'm in danger."

"Are you all alone, Romee?"

"God, I hope so," I whisper.

"You're alone?" the dispatcher confirms.

"Yes, but I think someone is here watching me."

I give her the address and wait for her to respond like, "Oh yeah, that place? It's haunted, don't worry about it."

But instead, she types in a few things and says, "My name is Jessica. Tell me what's going on."

I tell her everything, leaving out the copious glasses of wine. Regardless of the alcohol consumption, it doesn't change the fact that too many abnormal things keep occurring since I've been here. She hears it all, including the breakup and why I came here alone.

"A footprint isn't out of the ordinary," the dispatcher begins. "You haven't seen anyone? Heard anyone?"

"No, but I feel like I've heard someone in the house. I've searched so many times, but I've found nothing."

"Do you feel like you're in immediate danger now?"

"I-I don't know." My heart is pounding so hard it feels as though it's skipping a beat or two. The irregularity and intensity is making me lightheaded.

I've run up to the second floor, phone to my ear and the same knife I had overnight in my other hand. I'm on higher ground, but for what? I'm looking out the window—sans blinds—waiting to see someone, but I see nothing but more snow on the horizon. The rushing inside and upstairs is catching up with me, and combined with my erratic heartbeat, I feel as though I could topple over any minute.

"I feel sick." I sit down on one of the chairs.

"Ms. Anderson, the nearest patrol car is a few miles away, but as you can guess, the snow is making it difficult for our officer to safely get where he needs to be. We're also a little short staffed with it being Christmas Eve."

My heart picks up speed and expands, creating a tightness in my chest. I imagine the sharp pains crackling and popping inside my rib cage, mimicking the fire downstairs.

"Does that mean I'm screwed?" I ask.

"No, but there are higher priority calls our office is dealing with. There's been a minor car accident in town that needs redirecting, and—" she pauses for a few moments. "There has also been a skiing accident that has drawn a lot of outside help there. It's hard getting a snowplow up here to pave the roads for an ambulance."

"I just want to go home. How can I do that? I don't feel safe here."

"I understand, and it does sound very frightening."

A weird laugh comes out of me, filled with pity.

I don't want her agreeing with me. I want her to tell me there's nothing wrong and I'm safe. I appreciate she's trying to placate me and validate my feelings—even if I do

71

sound like a madwoman—but I don't want confirmation that this is actually a frightening experience to be in.

My baseline level will not return to normal until I'm in my own bed at home. This shortness of breath and current state of panic are here to stay.

"What are you saying?" I ask her.

"No one can be there for a while. Is there a room you can barricade yourself in if you truly feel like you're in danger?"

"I mean, yes, there is. Do I really need to hide?"

"That's up to you. Do you feel like you need to?"

"I don't know. I don't know anything. I'm freaking out, probably making this sound worse than it is. I'm so sorry."

My inherent people-pleaser characteristic is being brought to light for keeping her on the line over something so trivial. What if people are trying to call to report a crime or fatal accident? And here I am rambling along, crying about missing socks, a messed up blind, and a puddle of water at the door.

"Oh my gosh, the sneeze!" I whisper-shout.

"What sneeze?"

"Last night, I was FaceTiming my friend, and she heard a sneeze when I got up to get more wine—"

Damn, I didn't want to mention the alcohol, but it sounds like she doesn't care either way.

"Romee, this does sound odd. I will have a patrol car come as soon as he's available."

"Is that in...an hour? More?"

I lower the phone from my ear so I'm able to see the time, but notice "No Service" in the upper left corner of my cell phone.

"I don't have any service," I inform the dispatcher. "How am I able to talk to you with no service?"

"You're still able to make emergency calls even if you don't have a signal. Do you want me to stay on the line with you until an officer is able to come by? I can still answer other calls, I'll be muted."

"I don't know," I low-key wail.

I'm in my room now, shoving all my things inside my suitcase. The second the roads are cleared, I'm out of here. I'll risk visibility and sleet and drive two miles per hour until I reach safety. Even if that means getting into town and waiting at the local store until it's safe to descend the mountain. Maybe if someone *is* after me, maybe they'll be dissuaded if I'm around other people.

"You've checked all the doors? You're locked in?" she asks.

"Yes, I've never once left the door unlocked. But I feel like something is wrong. Do you think I'd make it if I walked to Frosty Mart?"

73

I hear her fingers clacking on her keyboard and an immediate, "I don't know. Unless you're outfitted with snow gear, I wouldn't chance it. Plus, it's two o'clock. It'll be getting dark soon. I think you're safest in the house."

I swallow a lump in my throat, unable to agree with her statement but recognizing her concerns as valid, too.

"Why would there be a random boot print near here? The closest house isn't exactly nearby, and why would someone be walking up on the property?"

"Could the owner be checking it out?" Jessica asks.

I want to smack myself for being so stupid. *Maybe* Linda came by to make sure I had dry logs. *Maybe* Linda has a size twelve foot? *Maybe* her husband came by? Her son? I didn't see tire tracks, but *maybe* they were covered by the falling snow.

"I'll see if I can reach out, maybe send her an email. I'm sorry for bothering you."

"Don't apologize, we want to make sure you're okay. I'll have an officer come by as soon as one is able to get through the roads. Call me back for any reason, okay?"

"Yes, okay. Thank you, Jessica."

"Okay, take care of yourself, Ms. Anderson."

"Thanks, bye."

We disconnect, and I look at my phone to remind myself that help is accessible and I'm not totally without options. I'll send Linda a quick email and ask: "Hey, just confirming you weren't lurking around your house while I'm here. Have you been messing with me because you're some weirdo that gets sick pleasure from scaring the bejesus out of your guests?"

But when I pull up my mail app, not only do I see "No Service," I see something else on my phone, prompting me to look out the window.

The outside Christmas lights are finally off, but for the wrong reasons.

Sometime when I was running upstairs and panic packing, the power went out.

CHAPTER 12

BABY, IT'S COLD OUTSIDE

"**N**o, no, no!"

Running back downstairs, the only form of light and heat are coming from the fireplace.

"Shit!" I stomp my foot because I feel trapped to the fullest extent. What the hell am I supposed to do now?

I'm in the kitchen, grabbing the welcome binder Linda left out for her guests, the one no one probably reads.

I flip to the page titled "In Case of an Emergency" and use my finger to scan the paper.

"'In case the power goes out...'" I begin reading aloud. "'In the unfortunate event of the power being shut off, there is a backup generator in the hall closet...'"

I'm at the closet door within a few seconds, expecting to see an ancient looking thing. Instead, I see more pillows and blankets.

"Where the hell is it?" I'm rummaging through all the shit in here, hoping it's hiding among the linens.

I'm back at the binder, wondering if there's a scavenger hunt attached. Did I miss something? Why can't I find it?

There's a yellow Post-it Note attached to the back of the page, like it was left there by accident.

A bright red check mark next to: Ask Greg to chop more wood.

An empty box next to: Bring new generator before winter guests arrive.

Then a big line across: Master reset code for front door one-two-two-three-three-three.

"Linda, you absent-minded bitch!" I scream at the binder, unable to control my anger. The house won't stay warm on its own forever, and the heat from the fire is enough to keep the living room comfortable, but for how long? Her stupid mistake could cost me a lot if I'm stuck here overnight.

My throat dries up and I reread the last sentence on the sticky note.

Jesus Christ, does Linda not change the code after every guest? What if the previous guests are still here?

So much for barricading myself in the upstairs bedroom until someone came to save me. Last I saw on the weather app, the low today is twelve degrees. I have no idea how I could survive that with blankets and

77

layered clothes. I could shed *all* my clothes and take a hot shower—the hottest it goes—but then I'd be wet and cold when it would eventually run out, and I don't want to expose myself to that. Do hot showers even work with no electricity? I can't even Google how a damn water heater works because I've never had to deal with something so archaic.

I'm at the kitchen sink jerking the left handle.

"Please, please, please," I cross my fingers and hop from side to side on my tippy toes, waiting to see if the water temperature changes.

The slightest increase from ice cold to lukewarm is more obvious than ever thanks to the frozen conditions outside. Steam begins to fill the kitchen as warm water pours out the faucet.

"Thank God."

Next, I check the stove.

It's embarrassing feeling so powerless without the help of a search engine to answer all my questions. But I've never been in this situation, and I've never been stranded in snow like this.

Usually when the power goes off at home, it's not for long, and it's not in such wretched conditions.

I have to take in my surroundings and adapt to this. I have no other choice.

The stove clicks on and flames pop out after a few moments.

"Okay, okay, this is good."

But is it? I'm not even worried about starving to death because I'm hoping the police officer will be able to get to me and transport me somewhere safe, or at best, drive ahead of me to ensure the roads are okay.

The biggest question is *when?*

I can already feel the house succumbing to the lack of heat as I leave the kitchen and walk to the warmer living room.

Wow, it's crazy how helpful the fire is. I throw on more logs, possibly too many, but watch them catch fire and grow in size. If I wasn't so fidgety, the clean, piney scent coming from the living room would put me to sleep.

What the hell do I do now?

My battery life.

I'm fumbling with my phone when I see I have fifty percent left.

Even during this regrettable time, I can't help but realize Emily would think fifty percent is actually good–it's half full, whereas I see it as half empty.

Do I risk putting it on Airplane Mode to conserve energy and possibly miss communication if the roads miraculously get plowed and are safe to drive?

No, I need to keep this on me at all times in case a signal comes through. And maybe the electricity will switch back on soon. This isn't life or death right now. Why am I assuming the worst?

If I'm desperate, I can go to my car and charge my phone. But I've heard horror stories of people who stayed in the driver's seat while the motor ran and died of carbon monoxide poisoning because their exhaust was blocked by too much snow.

Despite feeling frantic and distraught, I'm also parched as hell. I'm sure the fire is stealing all the moisture in the air.

My trusty Stanley is in the same place I left it, and I take a giant gulp of water.

"Stay hydrated," I tell myself, like I'm preparing for war. I refill it to the top and plant myself right in front of the fireplace, wrapping myself tight in as many blankets as possible.

"You, idiot, Romee. You had to come here alone?"

I shiver even in my cocoon of warmth.

Am I going crazy? Am I as unreliable as that stupid character in the book I read? Am I overreacting?

No, Jessica the dispatcher agreed with me that this is all very peculiar. But maybe it's someone messing with me. Some lonely hillbillies from this Podunk town who are bored and need some entertainment.

Maybe this is as far as it goes. Best case scenario, nothing else happens for the rest of the evening, a police officer is able to get to me in time, confirming the roads are cleared, and I can leave this godforsaken place.

An even lesser best case scenario? I'm stuck here until morning and nothing else happens. I mean, hello? It's Christmas Eve. The only person visiting tonight should be Santa Claus.

I draft an email for Linda anyway, in case it magically goes through, asking her if there has been any activity outside her cabin.

Now all I can do is wait.

Wait for the power to come back on.

Wait for the police officer to come check on me.

Wait for something horrible to happen.

CHAPTER 13

CANDY CANE LANE

An hour goes by, and it's been quiet enough that I almost fall asleep. The multiple layers of comfy blankets are helping in terms of warmth but not in terms of staying awake and focused.

The house is officially freezing. No matter how many logs I stack inside, I can sometimes see my breath in certain parts of the house, where there is no heat whatsoever.

I've done a quick walkthrough on the bottom floor, ensuring someone didn't leave a window ajar so they could come in later in the night—if I'm still here.

And now that I remember it, the mace in my glove compartment might come in handy.

Grabbing my car key out of my purse, I bundle up as best as I can so I can still use my hand on the bannister stairs and not slip to my death, and head out the front door.

Once I make contact with the outside air, I freeze in place. My bare face is up against some harsh, icy wind, and I wonder just how red my cheeks have become. The layers I added didn't make one ounce of difference. The snow level is to my shins, and I have to walk down the entrance steps cautiously.

Opening the glove compartment, I pocket the pepper spray and make my way back up the stairs.

The cabin might be the last house on this dead end street. I wouldn't know; I never drove past to see where the next driveway is. This cabin doesn't even have a garage, just an empty parking spot that lies parallel with the narrow street that is more like a one way road.

I was hopeful that maybe it was so cold outside, coming back into the house would make it feel warmer.

Absolutely not. There isn't even a huge difference between the interior log cabin walls as there is to those exposed to the air outside. Both locations have me shivering like hell. Now I can thank the exterior wind chill for my burning cheeks.

Other than constantly checking to see if the power is on or if my phone suddenly has a signal, all I can do is sit in front of the fire.

"Maybe I really am being overdramatic," I admit to the quiet house.

It's been silent for another hour, and the sun has all but disappeared now. I'm sure the starry skies are one of a kind out here, and I wish I was able to see it before I left. But the clouds have overtaken the upper atmosphere here, and any chance of sunlight has set in the west.

As the old saying goes: not a creature was stirring, not even a mouse.

I think my only hope at this point is that Santa Claus might stop by and I could hitch a ride on his sleigh.

Checking my phone for the time I dialed nine-one-one, I see it's been over two hours. I really thought someone would have come by now, so it's alarming that I'm still sitting here alone.

I decide there's no harm in calling again to get an update.

The tiniest bit of hope blooms inside my bleak existence when I hear Jessica's familiar voice.

"Nine-one-one, this is Frosthaven Falls dispatch, what is your emergency?"

"Jessica, it's Romee Anderson again. I was calling to see if there's any update on someone coming by to check on me."

"Hi, Romee. How are things going?"

"Nothing has happened since I last talked to you."

"That's good. We haven't been able to get an officer to your area yet. The snow is coming down quicker than the snow plow can clear it, and it's becoming difficult for anyone to drive right now."

As if her words were obvious enough, a huge gust of wind rattles the house, going so far as to conjure up the flames inside the fireplace like a witch is about to cast a spell.

Peeking out of one of the first floor windows, my stomach drops to my feet when I see snow swirling in nearly whiteout conditions. Somehow it got worse in a matter of minutes.

"Doesn't anyone have a snowboard?" I ask halfheartedly. "A snowmobile?"

"I understand your concern, Romee. Hopefully, it'll be quiet and maybe the strange things happening were weird coincidences. I still have you on my list as priority three."

"What does that mean?" I ask, worried that the further the number is from one, the less likely I am to get help. Does that mean I'm third on the list?

"Right now the skiing accident is priority one, and we have a few priority two situations that he will need to check out once the roads are cleared, which we can't gauge when they'll be safe to drive. But please rest assured, you are not alone out there."

85

I wish she'd have chosen a different phrase, but I understand her meaning. And I guess I don't feel completely helpless if I'm able to get through to her.

"The power went out, too," I add.

"Drink hot water. Stay in one room if you can, preferably one with a fire or one you can close off with blankets under the door. If you don't have access to wood, light candles, layer up, and try to stay active to get the blood flowing. There's no basement with a backup generator?"

"No, no basement. I haven't seen any stairs that go below the house. Linda's binder said there's a generator in a closet, but I think she forgot to bring it back or replace it. I'm using a ton of blankets, but I'm still freezing."

"You have enough firewood?"

"Yes, so at least there's that," I say, completely exhausted.

"Call me if anything comes up. And even if it doesn't, don't hesitate to call me with updates since I can't get through, okay?"

"Thanks, Jessica. I'll call you in a little bit, I guess."

"Okay, take care of yourself. Bye."

When I disconnect the call, I wish I had chosen to keep the line open in case something horrible *did* happen, but I need to save my battery life.

The only thing I can do now is read on my Kindle to kill time.

Until someone comes...

I refilled my Stanley with hot water, and I've been hugging it inside my blanket like it's a throw pillow. It's heavy and clunky, but it's doing the trick of keeping me one degree warmer.

It's eight o'clock, and most kids are probably in bed, anxious and excited to see what Santa leaves under the tree tomorrow morning. I'm still on the living room floor, grateful nothing has happened. I should probably go to bed if I'm able to.

I'll sleep in front of the fire and surround myself with my mace, a knife, and anything else I can get my hands on.

My hopes for a rescue have been dashed now that a good chunk of time has elapsed and the police officer hasn't arrived.

"Get some sleep."

My mom has probably called and texted a dozen times. I can only imagine the worry she's going through not being able to get a hold of me.

I grab one of the candy canes I left out on the coffee table and swing the loop around my finger in a counterclockwise circle.

Opening it carefully so I don't break it in half, I suck on the straight end until I make a perfect, sharp point. I poke the end on my middle finger. I used to do this as a kid, making a little shank out of the sugary treat.

I'm about to bite into it when I hear pounding on the front door.

"Jesus Christ!" I exclaim, my heart thundering inside my chest.

The police officer?

I set the sticky candy cane on the arm of the chair as someone begins screaming.

"Let me in! Let me in!" a woman shouts from outside, her fists slamming on the solid wood door.

I'm unsure if I should burrow my way into the layers of blankets I'm hiding in and pretend I don't hear her, or if I should get up and answer the door.

"Please! Please!" the voice wails, tinged with so much fear that I'm about to ignore all my gut reactions and unlatch the lock. "He's getting closer!"

My hand pauses on the deadbolt, the stranger on the other side unaware I'm two seconds away from letting her in. Is it the neighbor I met on the first day? I don't even remember what her voice sounds like.

Common sense gets the better of me as I stealthily bring my eyeball to the peephole and see nothing but...blackness.

I don't see the front porch as I gaze in the fishbowl lens. No haunted face of a woman inches away from ripping the door off its hinges.

It's been taped off or covered up from the outside.

It wasn't like this when I went out to my car.

"Hello? Is anyone there? Please, hurry!" Her fists continue pounding against the door as she says each word, the panic in her voice making me shake.

"Who is coming after you?" I croak out, wishing instantly I ignored her cries for help and let her try another house.

But whose? The closest neighbor is probably half a mile away. Plus there are no street lights on and it's freezing. But where did she come from? If someone is trying to mess with me, they're not going to come banging on the front door looking for refuge.

"You're home! Please, let me in! Let me in! Let me in!"

She and I are both terrified for our own reasons, but that doesn't mean I'm letting a complete stranger in when I'm already on edge and prepared for the worst.

"Who's chasing you?" I ask through the door.

"My boyfriend. He has a knife. Please, why aren't you opening the door?"

Her boyfriend. Is this the asshole that has been harassing me? Did he think she was the guest staying here but it was little ol' me instead?

He has a knife.

Yeah, well, so do I.

The knife is in my right hand while the mace is in my left, both ready to be used if necessary.

I haven't responded, and she's quieted down. Is he coming closer and she doesn't want him to hear her shouting for asylum?

"I can't see you in the peephole," I tell her. "Are you covering it with your hand? Come to the window so I know you don't have a weapon."

"A weapon?" she shrieks. "Are you crazy? I have nothing on me! Let me in!"

"Then come to the window, let me see."

I'm met with silence, an eerie, vacant silence.

"I'm not going to do that." Her frenzied voice has been replaced by a calm, measured tone that sounds *nothing* like that of a woman being stalked in the middle of the night.

My gut has already decided I'm in danger.

I allow a minute of silence to pass us by when she finally asks, "Are you not letting me in?"

"I haven't decided." I grip the handle of the knife, unsure what my next move is. "Isn't your boyfriend coming after you?"

My heart is hammering against my lungs so hard I barely hear her new, cryptic response.

"He's already in the house," she confirms.

CHAPTER 14

THE LITTLE DRUMMER BOY

My blood leaves my body in a quick, fluid release. I'm drained of energy and life by a simple five-word sentence.

"You're lying." I fight to hide the fear in my words, but I can't help but sway on my feet. I don't need her to confirm it. I know it's probably true.

The puddle of water.

The weird noise I heard upstairs.

The blinds.

My missing socks.

I have to free up a hand while I stealthily dial nine-one-one, so I put the knife down so I don't accidentally stab myself with it thanks to my trembling hands. I'm on the verge of puking, my body betraying me and shutting down. The alarm bells ringing inside me are warning me that my legs are about to give out.

"You really can't see me?" she asks again.

"No—" Before I can put my face flush against the door to confirm, I'm met with the screeching sound of a drill. My head flies backward as a metal drill bit penetrates through the small peephole entrance, inches away from piercing my eyeball.

"What the hell?" I scream as I see the bit retract, creating a clean hole that is now visible to each person on either side of the door.

"Damn, did I miss?" she laughs, the whites of her eyeball appearing in the circular tunnel.

This fucking psycho just tried to gouge my eye out with a drill. The pit in my stomach grows, and I wipe my eyes, first in disbelief and then to be sure she didn't actually get me.

I've seen plenty of scary movies, and I know the element of surprise is advantageous to either the victim or the killer.

So instead of waiting to see what she'll do next, I take the unexpected approach.

Closing my eyes and covering my mouth, I place the nozzle of the mace directly into the peep hole, and spray a healthy load of the noxious fumes.

Her previous screams of false terror have been replaced with true cries of hysteria as I hold my breath and continue covering my face. Even a whiff of this stuff will bring me to my knees, and I need to be the alert one here.

Adrenaline is pumping through my veins, giving me the boost of energy I might need to ward off this intruder. I'm at the front window, two slats bent down as I make out a dark figure scratching at her face. She's wearing a black ski mask that soon gets removed and thrown behind her in the snow.

She's blonde, but I can't see her face clearly. She's wiping and rubbing her eyes, the drill at her feet and a gun—

Oh my God, she has a gun. It's shiny and dark, in a holster on her side.

Could a bullet pass through an oak door? I don't want to know, so I run to the back door in the kitchen to make sure it's locked. I've checked the first floor a million times today, but I check once more to make sure I didn't miss a small detail.

"You bitch!" she screeches between hacking coughs that sound like she's about to choke on her own breath. I'm surprised she doesn't shoot through the lock and come in anyway. Maybe she doesn't want the neighbors hearing the gunshots echoing through the silent night.

Maybe her main goal is to terrorize me, to take her time because she knows help isn't coming.

But she's at a disadvantage… for now. The splat of vomit against the wooden planks echoes through the room as the unknown woman heaves and sputters, her guttural curses mingling with the sickening sounds of her retching and violent coughing. Just a wall away, I stand on trembling legs, paralyzed by the horrific scene I can hear but not see.

Could I take the chance and make it to my car to hide? No, I could barely last outside layered up. I'd freeze to death if help didn't arrive in time. Plus, I can't drive out of here. That'd be the worst choice to make right now.

I remember her previous threat of her boyfriend being inside. The house is dark enough due to the power outage, and the only source of light is coming from the fireplace. All the blinds are closed, so even if she *could* see well, she won't be able to see me going from room to room. And if someone is truly inside the house with me, maybe it'll be dark enough that he can't see me, too.

Her breathing is heavy and I hear pacing, the wooden boards releasing a tiny groan as she cries outside.

Do I check upstairs? Do I go on the offensive again and see what happens?

Instead, I find the darkest corner in the living room and hide. I'm draped under a blanket as I set the knife down and dial for help. My entire body shakes as I hit the send button and wait for someone to answer.

"Nine-one-one, this is Frosthaven Falls dispatch, what is your emergency?"

"Jessica," I whisper.

"Romee? Is that you? Are you okay?"

"No, someone is here. She tried to come into the house. She has a gun. She said her boyfriend is already in the house."

I hear Jessica typing away at her keyboard, hopefully changing my priority three to a priority one call.

"Can you find a safe place until help arrives?" she asks.

"You mean no one is around the corner yet?"

"The roads are still closed. I'll see what I can do. He can't get there on foot, it'll take too long. What did the female look like?"

"I couldn't see much, just that she was blonde. I'm scared to keep talking to you. What if she finds me?"

"I understand, Romee. But this is important. How tall? Any scars, tattoos?"

"Maybe 5'5? She was wearing a black ski mask. I can barely see anything because the power is still out."

In the brief moment I hear Jessica typing in this information, I'm gauging whether this woman hiding her face is a good thing or a bad thing.

If she didn't want me to identify her, maybe all she wants to do is fuck around and scare me. Then she'll be on her way.

If she was going to kill me, she wouldn't care if I saw what she looked like or not.

"Do you feel safe where you are?" Jessica asks.

"Absolutely not!" I hiss.

"I think we could get someone there in thirty or forty minutes," Jessica says, probably being generous with her guesstimate.

I cup my hand over my mouth and pinch my lips so hard a tear escapes.

Thirty minutes? If there really is someone inside the house, I'm outnumbered. Even if I blinded the woman outside, I know I'm at a disadvantage against a man. And she has a gun, which makes me think he'll be armed as well.

Jessica goes through a script of self-defense moves that I'm hoping I won't have to use. She says phrases like, "Palm heel strike, knee strikes, and groin kicks," all things that I comprehend for a split second and then forget immediately due to the building panic.

The house is quiet and unmoving, a complete contrast to the little drummer boy inside my chest, banging his drum so hard it feels like it'll give away my location.

Even the woman outside has fallen silent. Maybe I got lucky and she buried her face in the snow to alleviate the burning and she accidentally suffocated herself. Maybe the elements got to her. Maybe she was lying about her boyfriend–

But then, the sound of a door opening upstairs echoes the muted house.

My palm is back to covering my mouth when my suspicions are confirmed.

It's unmistakable: the gentle turn of the knob and creak of a door hinge. It can't be coming from my bedroom, because I put a hole in the drywall thanks to those greased up hinges. He has to be in one of the other bedrooms.

I whisper to Jessica through my fingers, goosebumps breaking out all over my arms and tears cascading down my cheeks, "Someone's inside."

CHAPTER 15

CHRISTMAS DREAMS

This can't be a robbery. Don't those happen during the day? Who the hell burgles someone on Christmas Eve? And what the hell do I have worth stealing? I'm a guest here and brought nothing of value.

"Remain calm," Jessica tells me. "Help is coming. Stay where you are, barricade yourself if you can."

There's no way the woman outside got inside from a second floor window. Even if she climbed a tree, jimmied open a bedroom window, in the freezing cold, and managed to do this with limited eyesight and lung capacity, there's no plausible way in.

So yes, that means there truly is another person, and he's already inside. He's come and gone as needed, most likely when I made the quick trip in town, checked my car, or fell asleep. The front door has a code but the back

KRISTIN MULLIGAN

door has a deadbolt. Does he have a key? The six digits necessary to come inside? I'm no locksmith, but goddamn if that ancient thing on the back door doesn't look easy to pick.

Think, Romee, think!

The man upstairs is in one of the empty rooms. The thought alone makes bile rise up my throat. I could vomit right now but I put a clenched fist to my lips. This has to be a nightmare. I'm dreaming, right? If I pinch myself, I'll wake up in my bed, and this will all be a bad dream.

Except when I blink away more tears, I know this isn't some figment of my imagination. I'm truly in danger, and I need to be ready.

My mind is spiraling out of control with every possibility.

I wish I didn't make that stupid fire. It's the only room that's warm, and the one place you'd expect to find me.

I haven't heard a floorboard creak overhead, which makes me think he's feeling me out, testing when and how he'll make his appearance.

If he hasn't left his spot, maybe I have enough time to prepare.

"I can't talk," I tell Jessica.

"Keep me on the line. Do not hang up."

Emerging from my hiding spot, I look around to make sure I didn't miss a third person lurking in a dark corner.

I stuff the phone inside my shirt and bra, with the microphone pointed out from the collar of my long coat.

Shit, I can't move well in this, but I can't take it off or I'll really be screwed. The cold will get to me quicker than they could. The coat stays on.

I carefully grab the fire poker and set the sharpened tip directly in the fire. That will make a nice weapon after it sits in that inferno for a few minutes.

I'm about to return to my spot when I hear the outside boards on the wraparound porch.

It's her.

And when I focus my attention, I can hear her labored breathing. Maybe she'll get hypothermia or frostbite.

The sliding glass door wiggles, causing a tiny yelp to escape my lips. It doesn't budge, but she continues to shake it anyway.

"There's no use hiding." Her voice sounds normal, not like someone who was suffering in immense pain. What if the pepper spray has already worked its way out of her system?

A floorboard bends under the weight of someone upstairs, and my hold on the knife tightens. I am not letting go of this thing until I'm out of here.

I can't even peek outside to see if the snow has stopped or if they have a car parked near mine. If they do, maybe the roads are safe enough to drive.

Could I make it to my car and manage to drive far enough away to flag down a neighbor?

But who can I trust? What about that lady at the store? She seemed nice enough; could my car make it that far in the snow?

Maybe I can turn on my car alarm to distract them both and sneak out the back door? But go where, exactly? My boots are waterproof, but they're not made for this kind of terrain, and I'm not prepared for the freezing temperatures. I'd die out there.

I tiptoe to my purse anyway, which has the lone car key. Instead of rifling through it in the foyer, I grab the whole thing and return to my spot in the corner.

I know backing myself up into a literal corner is not smart, but I feel like it's the only option I have right now. There's a bathroom downstairs, but I can't exactly pick up the toilet and block the entry. The latch will barely help keep me safe in there, and I don't want to be stuck in a tiny space with no other way out.

I'm digging through my purse, causing a ruckus louder than I'd like, but I can't find my key.

"No, no, no," I cry in near silence as reality hits me.

It was here earlier when I got the mace, and I'm positive I put it back. Did he take it? How did he do this without me noticing?

I wipe at my wet eyes, terror building inside me.

"They took my car key," I whisper again to Jessica.

I'm stuck here until help arrives—if the police even get here on time.

He has to be letting her inside soon, there's no way around it.

Which means I need to be ready.

Wherever the man is upstairs, he's staying there until they figure out a plan.

I need to be aware of him coming down and her coming in.

The boots I'm wearing are too clunky for me to move about undetected. I'd take them off, but I need to stay prepared in case I end up outside. I'll have to move carefully.

There's a bottle of olive oil on the kitchen counter, so I stick to the baseboards and walls as I make my way there.

I have to pass the staircase to my left as I enter the kitchen, and the brief thought of him barreling down the stairs has me getting blurry vision. My body is going to turn on me and shut down because it can't handle this unthinkable situation. This happens in horror movies, not to innocent elementary school teachers.

I tip the bottle upside down and let a generous amount of olive oil coat the wooden steps and banister of the lower landing. It's a surprisingly quiet act as the thick liquid seeps into the flooring.

I'm shaking as I drain the bottle, realizing he could be watching me from a dark corner of his hiding spot. My neck is throbbing as my heart thrashes inside it, poisoned with fear. Imagining some unknown person has been under the same roof as me makes me ill.

When I return to the small living room, I see the poker's tip burning bright red.

Perfect.

I'll keep it there until I need it.

That tingly sensation hits me, and I feel like someone has eyes on me. I swivel around and wait for her shadow to appear from a window, but I see nothing.

Find a safe spot.

I check my phone and see the numbers ticking by on the call.

"Jessica?" I whisper, fishing for the phone out of my shirt and bringing it to my ear.

"I'm still here, tell me what's going on," she demands.

"I'm on the bottom floor, living room."

Jessica says something in the receiver, but I can barely comprehend a word because the phone nearly slips out of my hand.

"I see him." I have to remember to breathe before I tell Jessica the next part. "He's coming downstairs."

CHAPTER 16

DECK THE HALLS

A figure in black emerges from around the corner at the top of the stairs.

Oh God, oh God, oh God.

The knife is still in my hand, and I don't think he sees me yet. The glow of the fireplace illuminates only half the room, creating pockets of darkness, like the one I'm hiding in.

I can't see his face clearly, but it doesn't matter anyway. He's also wearing a black ski mask, and the sight alone ratchets up my terror.

Do I know these people? Are they strangers?

A brief moment of fear eclipses me as I watch the figure move, hoping the familiarity isn't one I know *too* well.

Could it be Landon? Was I dating a psychopath and had no clue?

Will it be the stranger I met at Trader Joe's? Did he follow me up here?

I hope to never see either of their faces up close, but could it be Linda? Not that I would even know what she looks like...

My unstable brain is creating new nightmares, and I'm second guessing every interaction I had with any member of this snowy town.

They have my car key—*please just steal my car and leave me here.* But even so, they can't drive in this. What is their reasoning behind all this? To scare me? To have some fun?

The dark figure on the stairs looms over the top and begins to descend.

It all happens so fast. One moment he's at the highest part near the top hallway, quietly putting one foot in front of the other down the stairs, the next his heel is slipping in the olive oil, his grip on the banister slimy and wet.

He tumbles down the straight, narrow staircase, his body rolling in awkward, inconceivable shapes as he lands at the bottom with a massive splat. His large frame shakes the whole house as I hear him groan. Did I hear bones snap? What was that clatter?

A gun.

They're not just playing around. They are here to kill you.

The asshole is huge. His sustained injuries could be as minuscule as disorientation and a dislocated shoulder, or as severe as a broken neck or back, or dead.

But I hear a faint moan coming from his unmoving body, so he's still alive. His world has been turned upside down, and I can't imagine he's not seeing white stars in the ink-black house.

His partner outside had to have heard that, so I can't waste time contemplating if this is the right move. It's now or never.

I never imagined myself a killer, but dammit, if it's me or him that dies tonight, it's going to be him.

I emerge from my hiding spot and move fast. The knife handle is a new appendage, and I'm not letting go until it's being pried out of my hands when this is all over.

Sprinting to where this mystery man lies on the floor in the foyer of the downstairs hall, I'm able to make out the whites of his eyeballs peeking through the two holes in his ski mask.

My sight is adapting to the darkness, the glow of the fireplace aiding me in my quest for self-defense.

But it's also helping *him*. Because as I get close enough to strike, knife raised, ready to stab this motherfucker, his left knee retracts back into his chest and blows forward, connecting with my left ankle.

A burning sensation erupts in the muscles of my leg, shooting hot pain from the tips of my toes all the way to my thigh.

It's so unexpected and forceful, he knocks me down completely from the sheer strength he has over me.

My arms hit the ground first, my wrists absorbing most of the impact. I manage to tuck my chin to my chest to avoid my head hitting the ground. But most of the pain is radiating up and down the left side of my body.

My boot offered some protection, but not enough. I draw blood from biting my tongue to disguise the scream on the verge of my lips. The metallic taste stains my teeth, but I can't let this shake me for good.

We're both scrambling to get up. Him, looking for his gun, me, searching for the knife that got knocked out of my hand when I fell.

I'm disoriented from the pain, hunting for that knife, knowing my life depends on it. My eyes are stinging with tears, making this even more difficult. I'm seeing spots as I try to focus.

And for the split second I look away to size up the intruder, I have the urge to dry heave.

He's massive. At least 6'3. He looks solid and bulky, and I almost burst into tears when I realize how helpless I am. He's probably one of those horror movie killers who could choke out his victim with one fist around their throat, their body dangling from his outstretched hand like they weigh nothing. I momentarily imagine myself in that very spot. My breathing is coming in short, shallow inhales, and I'm going to pass out if I don't regulate it.

Deep breaths. In through the nose, out through the mouth.

I can't find the goddamn knife handle as I fumble behind me, desperately trying not to break eye contact with my assailant.

My phone got knocked out of my shirt, too, and I hope the call didn't disconnect. I want a recorded account of everything happening—whether I survive or not.

The stranger doesn't care that he's on his hands and knees, back turned, trying to locate his gun.

All he needs to do is get one good punch in and I'm done for. Lights out.

No, stop. Find something else before he does.

I'm ready to take off the boot on my uninjured foot and throw it at his face, but I find something better.

A useless floor lamp is propped to my left, so I rip the cord out of the wall and hurl it at him like a javelin.

My aim isn't the best, but it connects with his lower back in a resounding crash. He remains on all fours still, but his back bows with the contact.

That fall down the stairs didn't seem to do much to him, but he has to be in some kind of pain, too. Perhaps the adrenaline is masking the physical distress he's in.

I'm petrified to put weight on my ankle and find out it's broken, but I get off my ass and stumble into the living room, hoping the fire will reveal the glint of the knife I dropped.

A weapon, find a damn weapon.

The fire poker!

Its tip is radiating a beautiful orange-amber glow, similar to lava, but when I stand on my two feet and reach for it, he grabs a chunk of my hair and pulls me back.

I try to pry his fingers apart with my hands. It's futile, and I notice his damp hands aren't wearing gloves. He's not worried about his fingerprints everywhere?

One rough tug of my hair pulls me to where he wants me to go. I'm the puppet and he's the puppet master, in control of everything. My back is forced against his chest as he draws me in closer, so close I can feel his nasty breath on my exposed neck. He's exhaling deeply through a ski mask, the odor stale and musty, like he hasn't had the chance to brush his teeth in days.

Heel stomp.

I have no idea if I'll have any driving force with this, but it can't hurt to try.

With my uninjured foot, I crush the heel of my boot into the tips of his toes.

Nothing. Absolutely nothing.

It doesn't even elicit a groan or yelp of surprise.

His grip tightens thanks to that stunt, and I'm now at his disposal thanks to the pain of my hair follicles being ripped out of my head.

He jerks me around the room, taking me God knows where.

Next, as I expected, comes his forearm around my throat.

He's going to choke me out.

It's instantaneous when he flexes. My hearing goes first, the silence of the abandoned night screeching to a still, hushed whisper, and then to nothing. My vision fades to bright white as he crushes my windpipe, cutting off all my oxygen and blood flow to my brain. My screams are silent once his bicep tightens around my voice box, guaranteeing no chance of me yelling for help, as if anyone could hear me.

I'm fading... I'm fading...

The tunnel vision is closing in as the small black circle fades and fades...

I'm dragging my nails across his clothed arms when I should be saving my strength to combat this somehow. But it's useless. I'm kicking my feet against his tree trunk legs, hoping I might loosen his hold or knock him off balance.

I can't die here. I can't.

I relax and go limp, but press my back into his chest like I'm too tired to stand on my own. Using the doorframe we're passing through as leverage, I kick the wall hard with my good leg and the momentum sends us both falling backward.

He lands on his back as my near lifeless body topples on top of his. The back of my head smashes into his nose and mouth. The calamity works to my advantage, and the sound of a dozen eggs being broken all at once rings in my muffled ears.

"You bitch!"

He speaks, and I don't recognize his voice at all.

His partner has to be hearing the commotion from outside the house, and she will undoubtedly be joining any minute if he manages to unlock the door.

This brief moment is all I have.

Even if I'm a bit delirious from all of this, I can't lose focus on getting the upper hand.

He scrambles to his feet as I grab the first thing I see: the handle of my tumbler.

My forty-ounce Stanley is a bat, and his head is a baseball. I wind up and swing at that fucker as hard as I can. The sound it makes as it connects to his skull is like the crack of a home run at Yankee Stadium. It echoes in the house in a beautiful pop that makes my ears sing.

His ears are probably bleeding as his body goes slack and he falls to his side. His mask is soaked in blood, and it paints the walls in a Rorschach splatter, my trusty Stanley cup drenched red. A few drops land on my cheeks, but I wipe at them like they are nothing more than a few tears.

He covers his face with his arms, trying to protect his head like he's grappling with a UFC fighter. That didn't knock him out like I planned. Why couldn't I get lucky and find that fatal sweet spot?

He's losing energy, his breathing becoming labored and raspy. There's a muffled gurgle as he pulls off his mask to get more oxygen.

I'm waiting to recognize his face, but when it comes, I see a total stranger. Someone I've never met before in my life.

If I'm suffering over here, he has to be, too. A fall down the stairs, a broken nose, what more do I need to do to slow him down? He's hurt; he has to be.

The broken nose has soaked his face, the bash to the side of his head creating another wound that is oozing blood. He's shielding himself, driving his slippery heels into the floor and attempting to squirm away from me, his face a fucking nightmare getting worse by the minute. I even chipped his front teeth.

"I don't think so," I shout, staying close enough to fight on the offense but far enough that he doesn't destroy my other leg. I'm wobbly as I shuffle my feet, trying to regain my equilibrium after losing oxygen myself.

How is this asshole still conscious? I'm recovering from that near-asphyxiation, and my body is fighting to stay upright.

The way he's using his arms to block any pending shots also frees up his crotch area.

I stand over him and remember what else Jessica told me: *groin kick.*

Just as I'm about to end any chance of this asshole having kids, I hear the first of the six digit code being entered at the front door.

CHAPTER 17

DO YOU HEAR WHAT I HEAR?

She's coming in. I have to do this now to incapacitate him, or I won't get the upper hand. Maybe if he's too busy wallowing in pain, I can take her, too.

I drive the heel of my boot straight down into his groin, but my bad leg struggles to support my body weight, causing me to stomp his inner thigh and possibly his left nut only.

But the noise that comes out of him—oh my God—I can only *imagine* the agony as his screams ricochet inside the small entrance. He's rolling on the floor, clenching his genitals, when I hear the lock disengage and the handle turn.

Run!

Where the hell can I go? Upstairs? The tiny bathroom?

I break out into a pathetic scamper—given the nature of my left foot—into the living room as the blonde woman enters the house, gun tracking me as I maneuver in the dark.

But when I turn, fire poker in hand, my eyes adjust to a third figure.

No, there's no way.

The man is still blubbering on the floor, but my eyes aren't mistaken. *Two* figures dressed in black are standing fifteen feet away from me.

"I-I have to go to the hospital." The man is crying on the floor, howling like a wounded animal. "I think she ruptured my testicle."

I would smile in triumph if there wasn't a handgun pointed right at me. They're going to have to pry this poker out of my dead hands, if it comes to that.

I can't tell who the new person is or if they've been here all along...hiding?

The blonde woman sniffles, quickly wiping her eyes which are puffy and swollen. She hasn't put her mask back on. The third figure is the only one I haven't seen yet.

Who are these people? What the hell do they want from me?

The new unknown figure looks to be about the same size as the woman who was originally at the front door.

"What the hell do you want?" I shout. The antique brass handle of the poker is scorching my palm, but I refuse to let go.

"Drop the weapon," the one holding the gun demands.

"No, absolutely not."

Until they call my bluff and fire their gun, I'm holding onto a weapon. I'm not going down without a fight.

"Drop. It." She ignores the tortured cries from her partner on the floor, walking closer to me, but not close enough that I could clobber her across the face—which I plan to do, gun be damned.

My entire body is shaking, and I can't even hide it anymore. Even though I'm in an unimaginable scenario, I didn't want to let them know they've won. That my fear has amplified off the charts now that there are three of them. The hope I had for surviving this night is seeping out of me with each involuntary tremor.

I notice Jessica hasn't said a word, which is smart because once these intruders hear her muffled voice coming from my phone—wherever it is—it'll be over sooner than it began. I hope the call didn't disconnect or my battery didn't run out.

"How long has there been three of you?" I ask, trying not to sound obvious that I'm feeding Jessica details.

"Just the last hour," the masked woman says.

"What do you want from me?" The metal poker is searing into my hands and it's becoming difficult to ignore.

"Tie her up," the masked woman commands. This unknown third person is the oldest. She has a controlling, overbearing voice, and she's bossing the two around.

Mother and kids? Were they the last guests here?

The blonde woman approaches me, gun extended and pointed right at my chest. I could test how fast her reflexes are by striking the poker at her forearm, but what if I get shot in the process? What's the point of tying me up if they aren't going to kill me? Torture? The throbbing in my leg is killing me, and I'm balancing on my good leg to alleviate the pressure.

What's worse, being tortured for hours and dying anyway, or getting shot and maybe avoiding the suffering?

I'm given a brief moment of distraction when the man in the hallway releases a brutal and pungent gag. Bile and vomit, and possibly blood, soak the entrance floor as he expels the nastiest combination of smells I've ever witnessed. Both women momentarily look his way and I know it's the only opportunity I may get.

It's just enough time for me to swing the poker down onto her arm in a brutal, shattering impact. The gun slips from her weakened grip, clattering to the floor with a jarring, metallic crash as her strength gives out.

The third woman doesn't have a gun pointed at me—maybe she didn't bring one—and it's her downfall. As I run out of the living room, I wind up and take a good whack at her knees, ala Nancy Kerrigan style.

She screams, too, falling to the floor and releasing a string of curse words.

I'm internally wailing for various reasons. The excruciating pain in my ankle is compounding and multiplying. I have to switch hands with the poker because the faint smell of burned flesh might be coming from my own right palm.

Both women are bellowing like squawking birds, the older one shouting, "I've had it. Just go fucking kill her already!"

I'm limping to the kitchen, but not before I pass the wounded man on the floor, possibly succumbing to all his injuries. He might be dead for all I know. The vomiting has stopped, and he lies motionless in his own puke. It smells like death, and I cover my nose and mouth to hold back the bile threatening to come out of my own mouth.

The back door blows open once it's unlocked, a flurry of snow entering as I stupidly go outside.

But it's not without reason.

Footsteps trail behind me, and I falter when my feet connect with the slippery deck that wraps around the small house.

Am I even wearing layers? I feel naked and exposed out here as the freezing air penetrates through my coat. How have I never felt this degree of chill in my life? All those December mornings leaving my house and thinking, "Wow, it's cold."

No. *This* is cold. My joints stiffen as I maneuver around the exterior of the house, my goal fixed on the wall of tools for chopping wood. I seize a pair of hedge shears, their gleaming steel blades stretching at least a foot long.

I'm shivering so hard my movements create a clanging between the metal instruments.

Both women are hurt, but not immobilized indefinitely.

I'm crouched low below a window around the side of the house, and their voices drift easily with how quiet nature is at night. Aside from the brief rustling of tree branches, I can hear perfectly.

They're whispering, unaware I'm not far off into the trees most likely running to my demise.

"This is just like Mandy..." The younger one's voice trembles, skittish and in need of reassurance.

"This is not like Mandy. Take a breath and go find her."

The name Mandy sounds familiar, likely because before this trip, I researched articles to ensure this town wasn't some creepy place like *The Hills Have Eyes* or another horror film. I can't be certain, but she might have been one of the missing tourists who were never found.

Jesus Christ, are these crazed country folk responsible for that? I'm next if I don't find a way out of here.

Their hushed voices are even more difficult to hear.

"No way... He won't make it... Police scanner says... And streets are closed..."

She has a police scanner? Is she implying "he" is the police officer that is supposed to save me, and he won't make it because the goddamn streets are still closed off? Or is she talking about the man on the floor? This makes a huge difference for me.

These assholes came prepared with a police scanner, probably aware I called for help from the very beginning.

They know no one is coming to save me, and it might already be too late.

CHAPTER 18

CHRISTMAS LIGHTS

The fire poker is lying at my side. I can no longer hold onto it without losing feeling in my hands, and I need to be able to grip a weapon or tool without wanting to scream bloody murder in the process.

I turn both palms up and they are bright red. If I recall, putting ice on a burn could make it worse, so I refrain from placing my hands down into the snow.

If the women were smart, they'd both come out here after me.

I can fight one on one, but together? I'm not sure. My will to live might be stronger than their desire to kill me. I'm certain they want to survive this night, too.

I might have one down already, and he's my biggest challenge.

The older one sounds like she's in pain; her demands have a strained edge of discomfort. She's ordering the younger one outside.

The cold numbs the pain, working in my favor. I tighten my shoelaces around my injured ankle, creating a makeshift bandage to keep it stiff and prevent too much movement.

A light footstep crunches into the snow.

She's here.

Maybe the younger one got the gun back, perhaps she grabbed a knife from the kitchen, but I'm certain she didn't come out here empty handed.

I'm hiding around the corner, mouth inside my coat because my breath is still easy enough to see in the dark.

But then I have an idea. Instead of crouching low in my hiding spot, I wobble on my good leg so I'm in a standing position, and blow out a huge plume of frigid breath, creating a bright white cloud.

I immediately drop down to my knees and duck.

She's coming closer, and closer, and...

THWACK!

Two things happen at once.

For her, she slams an ax into the side of the house, barely missing my head. She thought I was standing behind the corner. Luckily, she missed my skull by an inch or two. Her ax head is jammed, wedged in the side of the cabin. The wood is so old, I'm shocked she didn't split the exterior wall in two. But the sound was deafening, and the metal hitting a pipe rings like a tuning fork.

For me, I thrust the large steel gardening shears into the top of her foot, the penetration itself hurting my hands when I connect with the wooden deck we're standing on.

She's a wild animal in the night, howling and groaning, stuck in place.

"Linda!" she bellows, and my already frozen veins turn to ice.

Linda, the goddamn owner of this place, is the older woman in the mask?

I'm consumed by a burning rage, a second wind catching me. I could probably fight off a hundred people right now.

Her foot is trapped beneath the shears, unable to move unless she frees herself and pulls them out from the wood, so I take this moment to really look at her face.

She's a stranger. Maybe thirty years old, someone you could see every day and never remember. One of my students' estranged mothers? One of Landon's family members? Why am I assuming something so outlandish when it's probably as simple as these Frosthaven Falls residents are freaking evil?

Was I the unlucky guest who happened to be in the way when a family of psychos decided to go on a killing spree?

My running imagination is interrupted when she lands a solid punch to my left cheekbone.

"Dammit!" I cower backward, shocked she was able to make such a direct hit when she's quite literally nailed to the ground. The pain explodes against my cheek, and I never realized just how powerful one punch can be. God, that hurts. She must have cut the inside of my cheek, because I taste blood and swallow more than I'd like.

I watch her contemplate pulling the shears out, her face turning white from shock. She tries to jimmy the ax out of the house, but it's wedged in there good and she can't jiggle it free without screaming and causing a bigger wound in her foot.

She doesn't have the gun, and it would be so much easier to shoot her. I really don't want to go back to the wall of tools and select the saw, quite possibly the only one left to use. That's messy, and face to face, and I don't think I could do it.

"You don't have the guts to kill me," she threatens, like she can read my mind. "As soon as my boyfriend comes to, he's going to pull every single one of your teeth out. Chop each finger off one by one. Or maybe he'll rip your clothes off and leave you in the snow, split you in two with his—"

I can't take any more of this, and Linda still hasn't come to save her, so I reach for the dead string of Christmas lights hanging from the awning and yank them free from whatever is securing them to the low-hanging roof.

The plink as each staple hits the ground is an indicator that I'm freeing up another strand of green Christmas cord, and I think I finally have enough when I pull with resistance.

I'm wrapping the cord around her neck, some of the large, incandescent bulbs breaking in the process from my frenzied act, while she lands blow after blow to my head and ribs like we are in the final round of a boxing match.

Shit, shit! She's getting some good hits in.

My vision turns spotty as I try to block her shots. My head absorbs a lot of jabs, and she connects with my ear, causing me to lose hearing for a few seconds.

But soon enough, I've run out of slack and loop it one final time as I hold onto the end of the cord.

She's not so bright, the act alone flying over her head. She's wearing a homemade noose, and it's too late for her either way.

It finally dawns on her, and just as she's about to pull the shears out, I deliver a front kick right in her chest, sending her body backward, fighting gravity in two ways.

She's essentially nailed to the floor, unable to free her foot, and I'm holding the bit of cord that coils around her neck like a snake, compressing her windpipe.

I close my eyes when she claws at it, her body contorting and convulsing as her oxygen is cut off while her foot is being split in half. She looks like she is in mid-fall, that move made famous by the *Matrix* movies, her top half being held up from the Christmas lights still attached somewhere on the roof, her lower half adhered to the floor.

Her face is bright red and appears to be inflating like a balloon. The deck is slippery with blood as her foot twitches and paints the snow red. Her neck is bloated and white, and I expect her to burst, but in a moment, it's all over. Her arms drop to her sides, her corpse limp and still.

I wait for her body to hit the floor, the weight of the Christmas lights snapping, but she just hangs there. And then the smell of excrement hits me.

I'm going to puke.

I lean over the railing, still keeping her in my peripheral vision, and throw up into the snow.

She's suspended in the air in the most unnatural positions, a vision I'll never get out of my head for the rest of my life, regardless of how much longer that is.

My hands find a moment of relief gripping the icy railing, the frost easing the burns, even as I ignore my own advice. But I ache all over; I'm in bad shape.

I feel woozy, almost drunk, as my senses start to fade. My vision blurs, hearing becomes muffled, and the only

sense that remains sharp is my smell—unfortunately, it's
the stench of death lingering in the air.

What am I supposed to do now?

My decision is made for me when the butt of a handgun
jabs itself into the side of my fragile skull.

CHAPTER 19

MY ONLY WISH THIS YEAR

"**G**et your ass inside. Now!" Linda demands.

I do what she says as she keeps the gun pointed directly at my face.

"In the goddamn house." She nudges the gun in the direction of the back door and I obey, sidestepping the woman I just killed who hangs like a marionette doll with a broken string.

I'm shuffling my feet while she follows closely behind. I'm trying not to highlight all my injuries, so I walk as best I can without revealing I'm falling apart.

The man is still passed out as I walk to the living room, slumped on his right side, surrounded by vomit. The stench is revolting, and Linda covers her nose with her free hand, also taking in the rancid odor. The man's face is still a bloody mess, and it's bittersweet knowing I might

KRISTIN MULLIGAN

have taken out two-thirds of this group, but it won't be enough to save me.

I'm shivering for a multitude of reasons, the most obvious being fear that my life is about to end.

"Are you hiding any weapons on you?" she asks.

"N-no," I stutter, eyes fixated on the gun, wondering if and when it'll go off.

"Where's your phone?" she asks.

"I don't know. It got lost when that-that man came down the stairs for me."

"That man—the one barely conscious in the hallway—is my son."

She motions for me to sit on the fireplace hearth while she pulls up the coffee table directly opposite me. Our knees are almost touching as the gun stays pointed at my chest. I wish I was sitting in the comfortable brown chair, next to the candy cane shank, but instead, my back is to the dying fire. I can't help but see the metaphor of the flames at my back, like death waiting patiently for me.

"What do you want?" I ask for the millionth time, wondering if she's here to explain this little game or if she'll just shoot me and be done. I'm not tied up, but I can't even wipe my nose without her finger going to the trigger.

"Well, it was supposed to be a bit of fun. We haven't had a guest here in quite a while..."

It's difficult to hear her through the mask, and this time, I don't want to see her face. It wouldn't matter anyway.

She picks up on my unease, also realizing it might be difficult to understand her since there are only two eye holes and her mouth is obstructed.

"Oh, let me take this off," she says, like we're out for lunch and it suddenly got too hot and she needed to remove her jacket.

She's quick about it, not giving me another chance to pounce, but when she reveals her face, I feel sick again.

"But-but..." I stammer.

"I had to see who the newest guest was on the day you checked in."

"But you own the big white mansion?"

"I do, but I also own this little cabin that rarely gets any guests. I think you forgot that my house is the first one on the street, so I see anyone coming and going. No one unusual has gone down this dead end street since you arrived. So I knew you were alone—no 'boyfriend' who was getting dropped off."

"So, you harass the guests?" My statement gives me false hope. You don't terrorize someone and let them go after you've killed their son's girlfriend outside. And once she revealed her face to me, there's no way she's letting me leave alive. I can't ignore the fact they are probably responsible for the infrequent and sporadic crime that happens here.

"Since it doesn't matter anyway, all you need to know is your car and body will be found at the bottom of a cliff. No one will know what happened here—"

Linda knows I called the police for help, but maybe she's unaware that Jessica has hopefully heard most of what's happening inside the house. There's a chance my phone is still on that call, recording everything.

Do I bother telling her, knowing she'll be caught either way? Would I have a better chance of living if she knew that, or would she shoot me instantly? I hold onto the fact that if I do die tonight, she won't get away with it. My death won't be one of those Netflix documentaries where the killer was never apprehended.

I stay quiet and let her talk, hoping I can think of something to get out of this.

"...And it'll be like you left and disappeared," she finishes.

"But the blood, the-the woman outside, everything! Someone will know. Your cleaning crew. Your fingerprints are everywhere."

"My son and his girlfriend are the cleaning crew. They're the ones who change over the house after each guest leaves. They haven't been very busy, what with the lack of reservations. Safe to say, I have that base covered. It's not unusual for their fingerprints to be in here."

I'm on the verge of tears, about to beg for my life, when I see the dark blur of a clock on the wall.

It's well past midnight. I made it until Christmas, and now I'm going to die out here alone. It's true when they say your life flashes before you.

All my students are sobbing, still too young to understand what it means when *Ms. Anderson went to heaven*. And my poor mom, she's going to hate herself forever for letting me go on this trip alone. Maybe Landon will even have a moment of guilt for breaking up with me and leading me down this path. Or maybe he'll be relieved he didn't come and add to the body count.

All that to say, I truly do not want to die. It's my one Christmas wish that won't come true.

A tear runs down my cheek, and I confess, "I don't want to die."

"Think of it as the wrong place, wrong time. If it wasn't you, it'd be someone else. My son has been *dying* to get his hands on someone like you."

"So, you're all just fucking psycho? Is that it?" My filter has disappeared as I grasp the notion she will end my life either way. "Your son is probably dying right now in the hallway."

"He's not dead. Last I checked he was still breathing."

"It's not like you can take him to a hospital. They'll know he did this. And what about the woman outside? How can you explain her death? It's all too much if I disappear."

"You think I haven't thought that through?" she screams.

But no, I don't think Linda has. I don't think Linda counted on me fighting back the way I did, let alone killing one of her accomplices. And she has to be lying about her son. There's no way he's breathing through his deformed face.

"Shut up for a minute!" Her knees are bouncing, as is her aim, bobbling the muzzle from my chin to my forehead.

She's spiraling out, the cold hard truth hitting her like a kick to her lungs. She's fucked. Whether I live or die, the only thing she can do is deny her involvement.

"Please, let me go. I promise I won't—"

"Say a word? You swear you won't tell a soul?" Her tone is mocking me, and another tear falls down my cheek.

"You can go back to your house, I'll say it was just the two—"

"And let my son take the fall for this?" She gasps that I would suggest such a thing.

"He might not even make it," I point out. "And I never told the police there were three of you. I said two."

I see her contemplating this idea, but she shakes her head aggressively.

"Stop talking!" she shouts as she uses her free hand to rub the side of her temple. I'd ambush her right now, but it could still send a bullet in my chest.

That goddamn fire is killing me. I'm scared my hair will catch and burn me alive. Or maybe my heart will finally burst and send me into cardiac arrest.

The fire pops again, and we both flinch. I'm grateful she didn't pull the trigger. She winces, attempting to rub at her legs but regrets showing she's also suffering.

The fear must be overriding everything because I'm beginning to go numb. Nothing is hurting like it used to. Am I going to pass out on my own?

I want to tell Linda, "Let's just get this over with," because my chest is the only part of my body that's not paralyzed. It tightens with each inhale, and I want this night to end.

Where is the knife I dropped? Where is my phone? Where did the mace go?

I'm racked with a huge sob I can't hide from Linda. But maybe my humanity will get to her, make her realize she's not capable of killing a stranger.

It does the opposite.

She cocks the hammer.

It's over.

CHAPTER 20

RUDOLPH THE RED-NOSED REINDEER

B etween the acceptance of this situation and the fire crawling up my back, I can't sit here much longer.

Might as well fight.

Linda's not as slow as I suspected, because when I lunge for her, her reaction time is immediate. The gun goes off in an ear-splitting blast, a bullet exploding through my left arm, ripping through my muscles and flesh.

We both collapse over the coffee table due to my propulsion off the fireplace hearth.

Another gunshot shatters my eardrums, hitting the ceiling above us. Her arm is now aimed flat above her head, but it feels as though it was shot right near the side of *my* head. It's so loud, disorienting me in the worst way.

Linda's below me as I straddle her, using gravity to pin her arm down and prevent her from aiming the gun at me again. She's firing it with reckless abandon, using up a bullet or two, trying her hardest to find *any* worthy spot on my body.

My coat sleeve is already soaked in blood, but I ignore it, using all my strength to keep her on the floor.

I should have the upper hand, I am on top of her, but she's stronger than I realized.

"Get...off...me," she grunts, thrusting her hips off the ground so maybe it'll propel me forward.

It almost works, my balance swaying as my left arm begins to go numb. It'll be pointless if I can't feel around, the nerve endings probably shredded. But it doesn't stop me as I fight to get the gun out of her hands.

Another shot goes off, and despite the alarm ringing inside me that all it takes is one good round in, I summon all the strength I have left.

I crash my bare forehead straight into the tip of her nose.

The crunch. The blood spray. The discombobulation.

I'm untangling Linda's death grip as she contends with a shattered nose while I'm trying not to pass out from the consequence of that move.

But when I almost have her fingers off the gun, she tosses it behind her into the hallway, so I'm unable to have it, either. I hear it skitter across the wood floor, stopping who knows where.

Now we are both defenseless, neither with a weapon but our bare fists.

Am I really fighting for my life against a woman old enough to be my mother? This is fucking asinine.

We're scrambling to our feet, Linda on wobbly knees, me clutching my left arm as I'm losing feeling completely. I'm losing blood, too. Fatigue is setting in and causing any movement to feel like I'm stuck in cement. Every limb weighs a hundred pounds. I'm thirsty, on the precipice of throwing up again, and confusion is creeping in.

What I wouldn't give to see red and blue flashing lights right about now.

It's a standoff, both of us vertical and waiting for the other to react. Linda doesn't go for the gun, unsure of its exact location, and she's blocking the wide exit for me to run to safety in another room.

My best option is to throw something at her, an act that seems so childish and useless, but it's all I have.

There's a small vase full of fake flowers, so I hurl it at her. She blocks it with her forearm, but it shatters on her from the impact.

She's bundled up, so that might not have even hurt her, but I can't stand here defenseless.

Linda has the audacity to spit a huge mouthful of blood at me, and I'm unable to dodge the nasty fluid. It lands on my cheeks with a wet slap.

I'm not against throwing Marv into the fire, creating an explosion and burning the whole house down, but I don't have my car key, and I won't last in the cold night.

Linda runs out of the living room, and in that split second, I wonder if I should chase after her, look for the gun somewhere in the dark living room, or hide in one of the rooms upstairs. Too many options and none seem to guarantee I'll live to see the sun come up.

She's not as quick as she hopes, her speed sluggish from her bad knees. I spot my Stanley tumbler lying next to the man in the hallway and—even better—the mace!

I use my tumbler like a bowling ball, sliding it across the hardwood floor right in the path of Linda's footfalls. She trips on it and it sends her down, right at the entrance of the kitchen.

Get to her before she gets hold of a knife.

I'm only a few paces away when I point and press the lever for the pepper spray.

Anywhere near her face is target enough, and her voice reaches octaves I've never heard as the chemicals seep into her eyes, enduring the last remnants of the canister.

Linda claws at her face, the instinct futile and pointless. She's a red marble, glistening from the tears running down her face and the thick snot dripping from her nose.

I'm scared to get too close in case there's a backspray to the vapors floating in the air.

I stagger into the living room, searching for the gun. My fingers spread wide, feeling for something hard and cold. When I finally grasp it, I palm the weapon and open the magazine to find two rounds left.

Returning to the kitchen, Linda is at the sink, splashing her beet-red face with cold water. She's still gasping for air like she's slowly suffocating, coughing and blowing snot from her nose, hoping for a brief moment of reprieve.

My right arm trembles as I point the gun, a rush of adrenaline flooding me.

It's not like the movies, where the body goes flying across the room with a massive kickback. I shoot twice, using the remaining ammo, one bullet hitting her collarbone, the other piercing the side of her head. Linda's upright one moment, then falling to the floor a moment later.

She's lifeless, hunched over in an uncomfortable position. I kick at her ribs to see if she flinches. She's still for over a minute, no sign of life coming from her chest.

Her blood spreads out in a growing puddle, looking black as night.

It's over. It's finally over.

CHAPTER 21

SILENT NIGHT

The house is quiet...finally. I can't catch my breath; my lungs are expanding too quickly. I'm going to pass out—it's inevitable. My body is wrecked, blood is seeping away, and my energy is drained. I need help, and I need it now.

As I push myself off the floor, I try not to put any weight on my left side. It feels as if that entire half of my body is detached. I can't move my fingers; my arm feels like it's fallen off at the shoulder joint. What if help doesn't arrive in time? What if the damage is so severe that they have to amputate?

"Who cares? You survived," I declare to the soulless house. There may be four bodies scattered around the house, but I'm the only one left breathing.

I survived.

I'm crying, tonight's events finally catching up to me. Deep sobs I was holding onto escape my lips with ease now that I'm all alone.

"Get it together. It's okay. It's going to be okay."

Grabbing the mug off the drying rack, I notice it's not the happy yellow I used on the first day.

It's blue.

Sometime when I was asleep at night, they helped themselves to water and didn't bother hiding they were using the other dishes.

I'm trembling so hard I can barely keep a steady hand under the faucet as I catch water with the mug, but I get enough for me to chug in one gulp.

I have a second and third glass and try to stay hydrated so I don't lose consciousness.

My arm is numb but also feels swollen, if that's even possible.

I think I used up all the mace, so I grab a chef's knife and wipe at my nose.

Silently walking to the entrance area, I hold my breath and pray the man is still dead on the floor. I can't handle another jump scare, so I'm relieved to see him in the same place he was.

Despite pinching my nose and mouth shut, the smell is so pungent I can taste it in the back of my throat. I fear it'll be stained in my skin forever.

What the hell do I do? Kick him to make sure he doesn't move or flinch?

I get to my knees, take a deep breath, and then jam the knife into his left calf muscle to ensure he's dead.

My hope was there would be no reaction, so when the knife penetrates his skin and he awakens like a zombie being brought back to life, it takes me off guard. He lunges for me like I stabbed his heart with adrenaline.

I'm scrambling backward, crab walking and falling over because my left side is worthless. I'm immobilized, unsure where to go. I only brought one weapon, and it's sticking out of his leg.

He's moving like he's stuck in quicksand, and my response time falters due to this unexpected reemergence.

HOW IS HE STILL ALIVE?

He's not on his feet yet, but he's propped himself up on his knees, regaining his strength and equilibrium.

If this night weren't frightening enough, seeing his mangled, swollen face alone would terrorize me for the rest of my life. His cheeks are saggy, covered in dried blood and open wounds. The side of his head looks caved in, a permanent dent in his skull. His nose...what nose? It's crushed flat, covered in blood and snot and puke. His eye sockets are hollowed out, dark pupils laser-focused on me.

I'm crying again, whimpering as I squirm my useless body to the living room. The fire is almost dead, and the room is darker than ever. I can't see or find anything useful. It's a nightmare come to life: the one where someone is chasing me and my limbs weigh a thousand pounds.

I'm near the leather chair—the one I took naps in, watched television on, where I'd read and get comfy—when he grabs my left ankle and pulls.

It's my turn to release an animalistic scream.

His vise grip around my foot sends a wave of agony through my entire nervous system. I'm going to die from this act alone. My body can't take it anymore.

We're both on all fours, unable to move thanks to all our injuries. His strength is dwindling, because I'm able to grab the chair leg to pull myself away from him, despite his weak constraint. When I do this, the candy cane I was sucking on earlier falls to the floor.

The pointed end taunts me, the tip sugary and threatening–like an ice pick–and I figure it's better than nothing.

I flip onto my back right as his looming body straddles me. His hands close over my throat, huge meaty hands that are slippery and bloody. But he clamps down the pressure, and it's instantaneous. I can't go through this again.

I have my right hand cupping my own neck beneath his grip, trying to create a barrier so he can't squeeze the life out of me before I get my chance. But I'm relying on my left, injured arm to do the job, and I hope it doesn't let me down, given the distress it's in.

Before he sees what's in my fist, I jam the candy cane's sharp tip into his left eye socket.

When I pull it back, the remainder breaks into pieces, the pointy end still stuck in his face.

He's flailing around, covering his face and crying into his hands.

End this, Romee.

While he's distracted, I grab the handle of the knife sticking out of his leg and wrench it free.

Blood squirts out in dark bursts, painting the floor with thick, viscous liquid.

"Die, asshole!" I scream in his face, jamming the knife deep into his head.

He's like a toy soldier that ran out of batteries, stationary and frozen as he falls to the floor in a loud thud. The knife wobbles in his skull from the impact.

I'm left shell-shocked and in disbelief.

Is it really over?

"Jesus Christ," I cry, shaking uncontrollably.

Three people died tonight. Three. But I wasn't one of them.

CHAPTER 22

I'LL BE HOME FOR CHRISTMAS

I spend the next hour crying in the *locked* small bathroom, bundled up with blankets but still feeling like I'm going to freeze to death despite escaping my planned demise multiple times. I won't feel safe until I'm home. Until the police come.

I found my phone and brought it in with me, hopeful the dead screen would magically spring to life. It ran out of battery and died sometime in the night, during the chaos of fighting for my life. I have no idea how much Jessica heard, but I hope help is still on the way. I don't think I can stomach going through their pockets looking for my car key and trying to drive.

After a solid sixty minutes, maybe more, I determine I can't survive the worst night of my entire life, only to freeze to death before help comes.

The sun is starting to come up. Christmas morning is upon me.

Something Jessica said during our call stands out.

She asked if there was a backup generator in the basement. I truly didn't know if there was a basement since I never saw a staircase inside leading down. But I never checked outside.

There's no way these people could have survived in some hidden tent in the snow. They had to have been nearby, close enough to come and go while I was staying here—especially since they helped themselves to water.

And then there's the boot print—it was on the side of the house.

Exiting the bathroom and standing in the entryway where so much violence happened, I stomp my good foot onto the floor. A hollow sound echoes in the silence.

So there is a basement. You can't get to it from inside the house—I would know, I searched the interior up and down.

When I make my way outside, I look for the imperfections along the wood beams. They look so seamless, and had I not known there might have been an outside secret door, I never would have looked for it.

It blends into the back wall almost flawlessly. There's no door handle, but I see the outline of a doorframe in the wood. I don't know what to do, release a lever, pry it

147

open with my bare hands, what? The only thing I can think of is pressing my palms against it and pushing. The force releases a hinge or some type of latch, swinging outward toward me.

There's another door when I peel back the first one, a heavy duty entryway that has another keycode access.

I'm trembling when I type in the digits: one-two-two-three-three-three.

A green light blinks, so I turn the handle and enter.

I'm met with a burst of trapped heat, a welcome reprieve from the numbness consuming my body.

There's a stairway down, but it's not dark like I expected. I see flickering lights and a yellowish glow as I limp down the stairs, all the way to the bottom.

The sight before me burns a hole in my chest.

Two sleeping bags, food wrappers, lanterns and candles, and empty water bottles are scattered among the generator and firewood. A large red gas can is next to the generator.

"Please, please…"

Two space heaters are already plugged into it, a lifeline for these assholes to survive the freezing temperatures down here.

I've never used a generator, but I see it's already switched on, so I pull the device that reminds me of starting a lawn mower and hope it springs to life.

Yanking it a few more times, I wait for it to jostle awake. Nothing.

"Dammit!" I scream.

The space heaters aren't working, and I really don't want to stay down here anyway, but I can at least take their lanterns up to the house until the sun has fully risen.

But when I'm turning on my feet, I see what looks like an electrical box on the wall.

"Please, please," I'm begging. I need heat. My body is going to go into shock from all the trauma, and the least I can do is pray for warmth.

I flip a long switch and hear a rumbling above me as the heater kicks on.

"A Christmas miracle," I wheeze, the irony and truth behind that statement ripping me in two. A sob bursts from my throat, the tears soaking my face.

It takes me longer to make it up the stairs, but when I enter from the back door, I can already feel a slight temperature difference from outside.

I sidestep Linda's lifeless body and drag my destroyed foot and mangled left arm to the living room. I cover the man's body with a blanket, then cover my own as my vision grows hazy on the couch.

Help is coming. It'll get here.

I pass out before I remember I can charge my dead cell phone.

149

It's the chirping of a patrol car that startles me awake.

I rouse with caution, my head swollen from the stress and strain my body has been put through.

Two car doors slam shut, and I hobble to the front door.

When I open it, a burst of wind chills the warming house, and two officers run up the steps and stop short when they see my condition.

"My name is Officer Phillips. Are you Romee Anderson?" he asks, disbelief radiating from his stare. He looks as though he's shocked to see me alive in the state I'm in.

I nod my head yes since I can't form the words myself.

They're late. Way too late.

"Call me Nick. I got the call from Jessica you were being attacked. Is anyone else inside? Is anyone alive?"

Nick, my savior, like Saint Nicholas. How ironic. He still showed up for me on Christmas Day.

I shake my head no this time.

"Where exactly are you hurt?" he asks, eyeballing my damage. My arm is shredded from the gunshot wound, and drops of blood that might not be my own are dried splotches on my cheeks.

His partner has disappeared to the body dangling from the Christmas lights. Radio chitchat comes from the receiver on his chest.

"One confirmed casualty," the voice says.

"I-I got shot in the arm." I point to the obvious wound. My face is hurricane purple, bruising, and covered in blood. "My ankle is sprained or broken. I don't know. I can't feel much anymore."

"An ambulance is coming. Hold tight. Are you sure no one else is alive?"

"I'm positive. I'm all alone here." I say it with certainty, an undeniable fact that this horrific holiday has finally come to an end.

EPILOGUE

AND ALL THE FUN WE HAD LAST YEAR

Ten Months Later

I'm leaving the main police station at the bottom of Frosthaven Falls, the one located in the same shopping center where I gathered groceries before my traumatic holiday trip. I'm getting horrible déjà vu vibes as I put on my sunglasses and step outside.

The weather is pleasant enough for October, with a cool breeze blowing strands of my hair loose, and I'm finally able to lift my arm to tuck some pieces behind my ear.

In the past months, I've spent a lot of that time in the hospital or rehab—long days with physical therapists, regaining my strength after battling a gunshot wound, a fractured ankle, and fighting against sepsis and multiple infections.

You don't always see the aftermath of horror movies when the heroine walks away seemingly unscathed and in a state of shock. In my case, I hobbled out the front door into the arms of two brave police officers who sent me straight to a helicopter that airlifted me to the nearest emergency room.

I truly don't remember what happened after that. It was a blur of my body shutting down and recovering from the worst nightmare imaginable.

But I'm in a much better place now—not just because of the leave of absence I took from school, but also in my mental headspace.

Just as the automatic doors begin to close behind me, I hear a woman calling out.

"Romee? Romee! Wait!"

I turn my back defensively, bracing myself for a long-lost cousin of Linda's, ready to take revenge on me for what I did to their family.

But when a cheery brunette approaches me with a bright, gleaming smile, I relax my shoulders a bit.

"Romee?" she confirms.

"Yes? Do I know you?"

"It's Jessica, the dispatcher!"

When it dawns on me that the person I could only recognize by voice now has a face, I practically melt into a puddle of emotions.

I bring her in for a deep hug—one symbolizing all the gratitude I don't know how to express in words.

"Thank you so much for everything you did for me," I cry.

She wipes at a tear when we separate—something so simple to do when you have the mobility of two uninjured arms. It took me weeks to finally regain my grip strength and months to feel like I was making real progress toward being "normal" again.

"I heard you were finishing up with the detectives, and I had to come meet you," she tells me. "I'm so glad I got to see you before you left."

While I never wanted to return to this cursed town, my case had some loose ends that had to be tied up, and it was just easier to do in person.

Linda's "big white mansion" was full of incriminating evidence. It turns out she wasn't as careful at her main residence as she was at the cabin she rented to one to three families per year. I'll kick myself forever for choosing it on a whim, but that's just how life works.

Linda was well-known around town for being the unassuming, friendly neighbor—a Ted Bundy in disguise. The only red flag was her adult son still living with her, which isn't so strange these days. Perhaps two psychos with a strong bond are hard to separate.

There was never a connection to the families staying at her cabin, as the infrequent deaths in Frosthaven Falls were never related. The few that appeared to be accidents—cars "driving off a cliff"—were actually the work of Linda and her son. The victims inside those cars were dead long before they plunged off the road, all thanks to the violent mother and son whom I ultimately killed.

Multiple bones and bodies were found on her property once the snow melted and they brought in a scent dog. Mandy—the name mentioned by the blubbering, stupid girlfriend I also killed—was one of the bodies identified six feet under the ground. Mandy never stayed at the cabin, but she came up with friends to ski and snowboard one winter weekend in 2020 and was never found. I'm hoping she put up a fight like I did.

My nearly fatal night may have brought about PTSD and recurring nightmares, but it also brought closure to many families who had no answers. Linda and her son were never suspects in any of the random cases of missing visitors or vehicles that vanished off the rocky terrain. In fact, the police are still searching for bodies that have never been found, somewhere along the desolate, snowy mountain range. I picture the scene in *Yellowstone* when they "take someone to the train station" and shudder at the thought of missing people sitting in their crushed cars, decomposing into bones.

"How are you doing? Did you ever get back with your boyfriend?" Jessica breaks my reverie with her loaded question.

I had forgotten I mentioned that little tidbit during my word vomit of incoherent thoughts on the first nine-one-one call.

"Oh, no. He did visit me in the hospital afterward to see how I was doing. He felt horrible but still wanted to stay apart despite it all. Maybe he saw it as a sign that we were meant to be apart, because who knows how things could have turned out if he had been there."

"But you're doing okay?"

I offer a simple smile as I contemplate how to answer such a straightforward question.

"I'm doing okay."

"I know this town is probably tainted for you now, but we really do get some good snow if you're into skiing. We'd love to have you back another holiday."

"As sweet as the invite is, I'm pretty sure I'll be home for Christmas this year."

"Well, good luck to you, Romee. Please let me know if you ever change your mind."

We hug one last time, and I turn to face the world.

Another gust of wind hits me, this time bringing a chillier aftershock.

A man rushes past me, a grocery list in hand, and says, "Better bundle up! A storm is coming!"

I look to the sky, where a dark gray horizon brings a sense of unease.

But this time, I take a deep breath, release it, and say, "Let it snow."

ACKNOWLEDGEMENTS

I want to extend my deepest gratitude to my readers. Your support and enthusiasm mean the world to me and inspire me to keep writing, even when I don't have a slew of ideas ready to share. Thank you for embracing this story and for your willingness to dive into the darker corners of my imagination.

Happy holidays, everyone!

Made in the USA
Las Vegas, NV
11 December 2024